The Nightwatchers

Candace Sams

Greenwood: Book 1

The Nightwatchers
Greenwood: Book 1

Whether we should fear or welcome vampires is up to us.

"I…I'm not like them. If I am, then you should have let me die," she gasped.

Sean pinched the bridge of his nose between his thumb and forefinger and tried again. "I told you. They're rogues. They look like they do because they've been eating the flesh of other vampires. They're pure evil. They made the choice to be the way they are," he insisted. "They sometimes eat humans if they can't find something they like better, like a changeling. They never had to live like this…they've chosen to."

When this didn't sink in, he tried again. "When you change, you'll look like I do. You'll have glowing eyes and elongated incisors…you won't be like…" He let his words trail away. She didn't seem capable of listening right now. Morgan was shaking so badly she couldn't move or speak. He was aware of her shock; it filtered through his senses like a jackhammer. For a moment, he felt compassion but quickly tamped it down.

"Come on. We need to get back to the compound before your playmates get the nerve to try again. I'll have someone ferret that bunch out and destroy them before they ravage the countryside." When he took several steps away and Morgan didn't move, he turned back. "Morgan?" he prompted.

She simply stared. Sean put his hands on either side of her

face. The posture effectively trapped her against the standing stone. "I'm sorry. But this is the way it is. If you can't deal with it, you can always stay outside and let the sun come up on you. I'm left with the impression it isn't a particularly pleasant way for a vampire to leave this life. But that's your choice."

The Nightwatchers – Greenwood: Book 1
The first book in *The Nightwatchers* paranormal action adventure series

Publisher: Candace Sams

Cover design: Candace Sams

Cover photos: @ Period Images, Deposit Photos

Prologue

What humans don't understand they fear.

Darkness has become a symbol of everything evil—where all manner of sinister forces dwell.

He was once as frightened by darkness as any other. Being human hadn't made *him* immune to that dread. But now that he was one with the night, and was no longer mortal, he saw things differently. What crept in shadows wasn't nearly as malevolent as a human heart bent on destruction. One single man or woman, obsessed with the desire to control others, was far more devastating than any creature crawling, flying or wandering through the nocturnal veil.

As a human, Sean Reilly had witnessed what lurked in the *daylight*. For him, what moved freely in the sun, under the guise of humanity, could be more terrible than anything his current existence ever presented. But he'd shoved what he'd seen into the recesses of his mind, deep down where it couldn't drive him insane.

No. The night wasn't evil. It was simply a force of nature—like him. He knew *true* depravity moved freely, out of the shadows and under clear skies.

Such malice, perpetrated on a bright Los Angeles day, was what currently drew him from his home in Ireland. And because of what had been done, a life would be forever changed. He was being sent to meld that life to the cleaner, more honest shroud of darkness.

In truth, he preferred the dark and all it held. Now, there'd be one more to share it—one more watcher in the night.

Chapter 1

Los Angeles, California

Morgan Grady heard the siren and her partner's voice as he told her help was coming, but she instinctively knew there was nothing to be done. As if in a dream, she heard the ambulance crew approach and the lead paramedic giving orders. The next thing she remembered was a line of white, overhead lights racing by as the emergency room staff hurriedly wheeled her down the hospital hallway and into the first available trauma room.

She was frightened even though the pain was gone, and her mind seemed to be disconnecting from her body. Someone yelled for a crash cart, and she heard a nurse calling out diminishing blood pressure numbers. She didn't want to die, but multiple gunshot wounds were difficult to treat. It would take a while for the doctors to determine which wound needed to be treated first, and she felt there wasn't much time left. Someone told someone else to ready her for immediate surgery, then she heard nothing more. Everything went dark.

After a time, somewhere in the darkness a familiar voice called.

"Morgan, darlin'…it's Uncle Patrick. Please wake up, angel."

At her beloved uncle's urgent request, Morgan forced her eyes open, and the pain almost overwhelmed her. Something must have alerted Patrick because she saw him stand, go to the door and plead for help.

"Please, my niece is awake, and I think she's in pain. Please…come!"

Morgan watched a white uniform speed into the room, though she couldn't see her attendant's face. Whatever they did to the IV dripping into her left arm, it only took the edge off the pain, but it was better than suffering the brunt of it.

"She'll need more than this, but I'll have to speak with

a doctor," the nurse advised.

The woman left and Morgan's vision began to falter, even though the painkiller had been in her system for just a few moments. "U-Uncle Pat?" she croaked.

"I'm here, darlin.' Hush now. It's goin' to be all right. I won't let anything happen to my girl."

Morgan tried to smile. Patrick Grady, her beloved uncle and only living relation, was always the same. He always saw the good side to everything, even though, in this case, there was no hope. She knew it deep inside. Facing her own fear, she desperately wanted to calm her uncle but didn't know how. His expression was a canvas of shocked relief mixed with dark foreboding. Still, it was so good to hear the soft, lilting Irish accent one more time. "When did you get here?" she whispered.

"I've been here for hours, love. Your supervisor called me, and I came right away. There are dozens of police officers outside, in the hallway." He put out his hand and gently touched her forehead. "You came through surgery right as rain. Everything is going to be all right now. You'll see."

He was lying. If the pain in her body hadn't given the fact away, his expression surely did. She lifted her right hand to try and touch his handsome face. At fifty-eight years of age, Patrick was one of the finest looking men she knew. He'd always been a hero to her, and she didn't want to be the source of pain for him now. Even though her intent was to show courage, she was more frightened than she'd ever been. When she felt his warm grasp around her hand, it momentarily helped her rally.

"Now listen, Morgan dear. You just rest. Don't try to talk or worry over anything. Your Uncle Pat is going to take care of you."

Despite her initial need to calm him, she couldn't hold back any longer. Her fear finally spilled over. "I-I'm afraid," she stuttered. "What's on the other side, Uncle Pat? What will it be like?" Despite her best efforts to seem brave, Morgan's soul lurched. She didn't want to die. She wasn't ready. At twenty-nine, she'd only started experiencing the big picture of life. Even her Catholic upbringing didn't calm her doubts as to what lay beyond.

"Hush now." Pat lifted her hand to his lips and kissed it. "I won't leave you. And you're not going anywhere. I told you I'd take care of it and I will."

"I-I'm such a c-coward," she blathered and tried not to cry.

"You're no such damned thing! Cowards don't do what you do. And I won't hear another word on the subject. Are you listening?"

She swallowed and attempted to nod. "You won't go?"

"You know I won't, angel. I'll stay as long as you need me."

She gripped his hand as hard as she could. "Will you do something for me?"

"Anything you want, my girl. *Anything*."

"Will you light a candle for me?"

"You'll be lighting your own candles…you'll see."

"I love you, Uncle Pat."

"I love you, too, my sweet, sweet, darlin'." He paused and sat on the edge of the bed. "Now, I want you to listen to me…I'm going to tell you a story."

She smiled though tears blurred her vision. "Like the ones when I was little? About Ireland?"

Patrick gripped her hand with both of his. "This one is a little different. But you have to listen very carefully, all right?"

Morgan stared into his dark eyes and nodded.

"Now…a long time ago, there were some people with special powers. They were unusual people, not like you or me. And they could actually change into animals. They could turn themselves into bats and wolves, and they lived by night."

"Like vampires?" Morgan asked. The pain medication was winding through her system now, but she wanted to hear

Patrick's story. She fought the meds and clung to every word he uttered.

"Try to stay awake just a little while longer, Morgan. You've got to hear this."

Morgan opened her eyes wider and felt him grip her hand with force.

Patrick continued with the story. "These men and women were *good*. Not evil as they're depicted in the movies. In fact...they were so righteous they tried to help right some of the wrongs in the world."

"Like police?" Morgan murmured and tried to fight off drowsiness.

"Aye, like the police...but they've existed for a very long time. And they live all around us now. They're still trying to ferret out those vermin in the world who would strike terror into the hearts of humankind. They're with us still," Patrick claimed.

She realized he was trying to tell her *anything* to take

her mind off the inevitable. Just the sound of his low Irish brogue made her feel a little better. But only a little.

"What if you could be like them, Morgan? What if one could walk right into this room right now and undo all the harm done to you? Wouldn't that be something, my girl?"

Morgan tried to smile. "Yeah, Uncle Pat. That would be something."

"You could finally go see the old country and…and be good as new."

Morgan began to cry in earnest. "Please hold me, Uncle Pat."

Patrick leaned forward and carefully wrapped his arms around her. "Don't you cry now, darling. They'll come for you. My friends from *Night Watch* will come. It's a secret agency…where *real vampires exist.*"

Something in her brain began to confuse legends he'd told her as a child with what he was telling her now. Nothing made sense. "Will I really get to see Ireland?"

"I swear, Morgan, you'll see and do things you've never imagined. You just leave it to me. But you have to want to live. You have to fight a little while longer. Can you do that?" He pushed the operating room bonnet from her head and stroked her hair.

"I'll try. But I don't—" Her breath caught in her throat, and she felt the air leave her lungs. The room began to circle, and she experienced light-headed illusions. It was as though her soul was leaving her body. She actually began to float up and felt the remnants of pain drift away.

"*Nurse*!" Pat yelled.

From high above, detached and unconcerned, Morgan watched medical personnel run into her room. They had equipment she knew was meant to save her life. A bright light began to glow behind her, and she turned toward it. Somehow, she didn't want to go there. She resisted. *Not yet. I've got things to do.*

***

Sean Reilly, formerly known by the surname *Murphy,* impatiently waited for the sun to go down so he could open the airplane door. As the last moments of daylight slipped away, he shoved the hatch forward and noted the stairway was in place for his descent. He could have easily leapt to the ground, but that would certainly have caused unwanted attention from nearby ground crews. He knew Danielle had already gone ahead, and the situation should have been like a dozen others he'd encountered. This time…*something* wasn't right. He could feel it down to the last drop of his cold blood.

"You'll have to hurry, sir. Our people have her isolated in a wing now, and the doctors have been told we're on urgent government business. Our own doctor is present so civilian personnel will cooperate. But she's in a bad way. They don't think she'll make it through the night," the pilot warned.

Sean nodded at the man and glanced at the waiting limo. "Get the plane refueled and ready to take off as soon as possible, Thomas. I don't want to stick around any longer than

I have to." It wasn't as if he needed to give the order. Thomas knew his job. But he just wanted to press the point; that he disliked his present surroundings.

"Problem sir?"

"You know me and cities," Sean replied and slanted a grin at the pilot.

"Yes sir. I'll have everything ready, including the blood. There'll be enough for two."

"Good." Sean turned toward the ramp but paused and addressed Thomas once more. "Any word from Patrick?"

"I only know he met Danielle earlier in the day. They were supposed to pick up some clothing at the woman's apartment, then meet you at the hospital."

Sean nodded, descended the ramp, and strode to the limousine. Once inside, he used his cell phone and dialed Danielle's number. When there was no answer, his sense of insecurity grew. Danielle always stayed in touch. Of course, this situation was different from any they'd encountered before. Naturally, Dani would want to have some time alone with Patrick, but their newest member of the organization awaited her fate. The fact that it was Patrick's niece *did* make a difference, however. It must have been very difficult for the older man to watch his only living relative drift so close to death, and realize she'd be joining the ranks of *The Nightwatchers* before the sun came up again.

It was almost nine o'clock before he arrived at the large Los Angeles hospital. It looked like hundreds of others he'd seen so he ignored anything humans had done to make it appear less like a place where the sick, injured, and dying were transported. All he cared about was that procedure was followed, no one at the hospital got in the way, and that the woman was removed immediately once she was pronounced dead. He would take her back to Dublin and train her just enough to let someone take over the task. Then *his* assignments could take precedence. He was only engaging this underling's job for Patrick's sake. The man had asked for him *personally*. Because of their long-standing friendship, he felt obligated to accept. No matter how he tried to shake off the feeling, something about the entire situation still didn't feel right. He wanted the chore over with as soon as possible.

Walking down the hospital hall, he noted familiar American human members of the organization standing guard. One of them motioned to him and opened the door to a room where a *Nightwatchers* physician stood by. The doctor and several other agency operatives surrounded a bed where his *initiate* lay. The equipment keeping her alive was still attached to her body.

"Where is her uncle?" Sean asked as he glanced around the room and saw neither Patrick nor Danielle were there yet. He couldn't sense their presence near the room, and it seemed strange that Patrick wouldn't be present when the doctor shut off the life support, and his niece was changed into a creature of the night.

"Pat is on his way," the doctor responded as he looked

up from his patient's chart. "But I don't think we can wait. Her vital signs have been slipping at an alarming rate. You have to do this before she actually dies."

Sean was perfectly aware of this fact. But Patrick and Danielle had more than ample time to have collected what little the woman would need and get to the hospital. Their absence wasn't right—especially Danielle's. Any time a woman was initiated, a female member of the organization was always present. He preferred it to be someone he trusted.

He walked forward and stared at the woman on the bed. A surgical cap still covered her head. An IV dripped fluid into the vein of her left arm. Half a dozen of other pieces of equipment hummed in the background, but he knew none of them could save her life. "How many bullets did she take?"

"Five," the doctor responded. "We had to take her back into surgery yesterday. I don't mind telling you she's a mess inside. God only knows what kept her alive this long. Since Patrick wanted you, we've done the best we could to keep her going until you arrived."

Sean leaned closer to the figure lying before him. He'd been briefed on all the specifics, but nothing prepared him for the perfect beauty on the bed. She was too pale but stunning all the same. "She's a fighter. I can sense it." He shook his head in remorse. "It's a bloody damned shame a good police officer ends up like this!"

"Her department has been told the same story we gave the hospital staff…that this is a matter of national security; we're members of the CIA, and they're to stay away. Everyone with an interest in the case will be told she was cremated. No one will know anything about us transporting the body to the airport. Our people will be covering all the entrances and exits. Security tapes here and along the route to the airport will be discarded."

Sean glanced at the doctor and nodded. This was routine, the way these things were usually handled. But it was recited anyhow as procedure required. He placed one hand on the woman's cheek. According to what he'd been told, she was only twenty-nine, and Pat had been training her for induction into the organization as a *human* operative. Sadly, she was shot down before the initiation could take place.

Her record was outstanding. Had it been more difficult for some drug dealer to get his hands on an assault weapon, the woman might have enjoyed a long, productive life. Things being what they were, the same attention she gave to her work would make her a good operative for the organization. If she'd been conscious, he would have asked her some questions and introduced himself. The drugs the doctors had induced let her rest peacefully. Without them, damage from the bullets would have inflicted untold agony. He recalled his own entrance into the world of the *undead*. Their inductions were sadly similar.

He glanced at the clock. "I'll wait for Patrick as long as I can. I need to get more information from him…personal information about her life. I don't like to just change someone without knowing something other than what the forms require."

The doctor opened his mouth to respond, but whatever the man might have said was forever lost. An alarm on a monitor went off and a flurry of activity began. Sean backed away so the doctors could get to their patient. He glanced at the door again. Instinct told him there was no time left. He had to take her now…or let her die.

"We can't wait," the doctor abruptly confirmed.

Sean pushed through the personnel. "Get this equipment off her. She won't need it anymore." He waited for the staff to unhook all the life support paraphernalia, then turned to them. "Get out unless you want to watch. This is *my* show from here on."

"Hurry," the doctor quickly advised, "she won't last long."

Sean riveted his eyes on the pale woman while the attending physician and agency staff left the room. "I'm sorry your uncle isn't here," he whispered. Then he sat on the side of the bed, quickly turned her face away, and exposed her neck. The visible pulse in her carotid artery was already slowing. He leaned forward, opened his mouth, and his incisors extended. When he sank them into her tender flesh, she softly cried out and lurched upward. He wrapped his arms around her to keep her slender body steady.

He then disengaged and repeated the same contact twice more. On the third bite, he heard the breath leave her body and knew life for her would never be the same.

As expected, her body remained still as he gently took some surgical gauze and wiped blood droplets off her neck. The surgical cap had slipped from her head, and long, light brown hair surrounded her exquisite face. It draped over the pillow as if blown there by a breeze. He paused a moment, then gently stroked a soft strand of it away from her cheek.

By this time tomorrow, her friends and colleagues would all believe she was dead. For her, a whole new life was about to begin; one where she might do more good than in her former occupation as a Los Angeles police officer. She was being given a rare chance. Perhaps, after his initial training, their paths would cross again. This would certainly suit him. She was one of those women others referred to as a *classic beauty*. Her toned body, high cheekbones, and full lips tempted him. The woman's utter helplessness stimulated protective instincts invoked by his having changed her.

He quickly tamped down these sensual threads of emotion and focused on the business at hand. Waiting for the *handling* and *delivery* sequence to unfold was always tedious.

He knew Danielle would show up with a few of the woman's belongings, and that his initiate's body would be placed in an appropriate container. It would then be escorted to the plane at the same time as he was being driven back to the airport. After the *changing* body was placed in the plane's passenger compartment, they'd fly to Dublin. He'd be required to offer initial training, but then the woman would be handed over to recruitment personnel. These events wouldn't take long. They'd been carefully orchestrated to maintain the organization's secrecy and to quell any objections presented by various governmental agencies.

He crossed his arms over his chest and knew it would only be a matter of hours before she'd wake. He recalled his own awakening and remembered how strange everything had seemed. The man who had changed him had long since retired, but the bloke been a good instructor. The training then had been hastily conducted because of the war. His tutor's presence was necessary behind enemy lines. Much of what he had learned, therefore, was on the run. At least this woman would have a protracted induction time.

"*Morgan*. The name suits you," Sean softly murmured as he stared down at the death-like figure. "I wish Patrick could have been here for you, but no matter. I'm sure he'll come soon." Even as he said the words, Sean sensed commotion outside the door. He stood just as Patrick Grady entered the room.

"Is she…is it *done*?" Patrick choked out as he half-stumbled toward the bed.

Sean slowly nodded and forgave Pat for not offering a greeting. The older man was clearly concerned for his niece. When the door opened again and Danielle quietly entered the room, however, the look on his assistant's face immediately alerted him. "What is it, Dani?"

"I'll let Patrick explain," she murmured.

Sean hadn't seen Patrick in many years. Even though the one-time field agent had aged gracefully since his retirement, it was still a shock to see how much older Pat actually was. This was the one thing Sean never got used to—watching the human members of *The Nightwatchers* age while he stayed thirty-five forever. "What's Danielle talking about, Patrick? What's there to explain?"

"I…I'm sorry, Sean," Patrick began, "I should have gotten here sooner. Danielle wanted me to, but I knew you'd figure out the truth if you started asking questions. So…I stayed away until it was over."

"*What* truth, Patrick? What are you trying to tell me?" He walked toward the older man, and the creeping sense of foreboding he'd felt after landing at the airport became full-fledged fear.

Patrick took a deep breath before speaking "She…Morgan didn't accept being inducted. She never agreed to any of this."

A vampire's blood normally ran cold. But never had Sean's run icier. He grabbed the older man's shirt and roughly pulled him forward. "*What*? What the hell are you telling me?"

"When the doctors said she wouldn't make it, I told Morgan about vampires. That was after her first surgery and when she was coherent enough to listen. Of course, she thought I was filling her h-head with nonsense…that I was just trying to keep her mind off the p-pain. I'm sure she didn't believe a word I said, but I knew s-she'd die if not for you. And I…I couldn't let that happen!" Patrick shakily asserted. "She's all I've got. And even if I never see her again, at least I'll know she's not dead. Her only chance was to let the organization think she was willing to be recruited. I knew she fit the profile so I called in the initiation. *You* were the vampire I wanted for this," he finished.

"Are you *insane*? Do you know what could happen to you for violating procedure? And *me* for helping you?" Sean's grasp on the older man's shirt never loosened. He shook him to make his point.

Danielle moved quickly forward and pulled at Sean's arm. "Let him go, Sean. I can swear you never knew Morgan didn't agree to this. I didn't know, either. Patrick doesn't care what you do to him as long as Morgan is safe. That was the whole point. What's done is done. We have to get Morgan on the plane before she awakens. We can deal with all this later."

"Damn you, Patrick!" Sean glanced at the body lying

on the bed. "Despite Danielle's assurances to the contrary, my ass is on the line. When your niece wakes up as a vampire, she might take *exception* to it. Maybe she'll even want revenge," he raged and then continued to vent. "The easiest way for her to get it is to tell the people in charge we've taken her without permission. The organization won't care about excuses. They'll want to know why I didn't verify your recruitment…why *I* blindly trusted a man I thought was a friend. And they'll want to know why we endangered the other operatives and the entire organization," he shook the older man harder. "Now, maybe you don't give a damn what happens as long as your precious niece survives, but I don't relish the idea of being staked out on a hill while the sun comes up. And did you even *consider* what would happen to Danielle?" he asserted. "As my assistant, she could also be held responsible. You know the damned rules, Patrick! Nobody gets changed unless they're willing and unless they understand the consequences and the commitment to the organization."

Patrick gripped Sean's shoulders. "Trust me, old friend. I know my niece. She *will* accept her place in *The Nightwatchers*. If you're half the man you ever were, you can convince her this is for the best," he vowed. "Morgan was a good cop. I'm damned certain she didn't want to end up a corpse…she'll come around. And you'll have one of the best agents the organization has ever known. You've seen her file."

"We can hash this out later," Danielle insisted. "Let's get Morgan on the plane and off to Ireland."

"Dani, this crazy man has just doomed his own niece to an eternal life she might not want. And he may have just gutted us as well." Sean ran one hand through his hair, then clenched the same hand in anxiety.

"I happen to believe him, Sean. Patrick should know his own niece. She'll accept this when she knows her life would have been over otherwise. Now…everyone calm down and let's get back on schedule," Dani quietly reasoned. "I'm going to call Thomas and tell him we're coming. I'll get the container crew in here and have them remove Morgan. Then I'll help escort her body to make sure everything goes as planned. Patrick will stay in Los Angeles and see that our cover stories stay solid."

Sean stared at her. "Dani, you're covering for him because you two are in love. You've both let your objectivity go straight to hell."

Danielle glared at her supervisor. "That's a space we'll all be sharing if you don't convince Morgan she's better off than rotting in a grave!"

"May the *Holy Mother* damn the both of you!"

Sean turned his back on them and ran a hand over his face. He paced while the two older people went about the business of carting Morgan's seemingly lifeless body out of the hospital. Only when he had his rage and thoughts under control did he leave the room and make his way to a waiting limousine.

***

"Thomas is ready for takeoff," Dani informed Sean. "Are there any instructions?"

Sean took off his long, black duster and threw it over one of the cabin chairs. "No. At least Thomas is *one* member of my team who knows how to follow procedure." He turned around and stared pointedly at Danielle.

"Don't be so petulant! We can't undo this," Dani remarked.

"Where is she?"

Danielle glanced behind her, toward the regally appointed bedroom that happened to be Sean's private resting place.

"You and Thomas put her in *my* bed?" he blurted.

"Well, she couldn't very well wake up in the coffin we loaded her into at the hospital, could she? It would scare the bloody hell out of her."

Sean snorted. "If she'd been properly instructed, she'd

know where she was and what was happening. Thanks to her uncle, she'll wake up on an airplane with a stranger hovering over her…en route to another bloody country."

Danielle clasped her hands together. "Would you rather I handle this? I don't see you being tactful in your present mood."

Sean lifted one hand and shook his head. "No. Stay in your section of the plane until I call you. Since my ass is in a sling over this, I'll take it from here."

Danielle sighed, waved one hand in a frustrated gesture, and walked toward the front of the airplane.

"I'll leave your cabin sealed unless you signal. Obviously, we'll have to stop and refuel, but Thomas has made sure everything you need is within reach. Morgan's suitcases are beside the bed. I'm sure that having some of her belongings will make all this less intimidating."

Sean tilted his head and watched Dani walk away.

If his assistant thought that having a few niceties from

Morgan's old life was going to diminish what they'd done, then Dani wasn't thinking rationally. Just as Patrick Grady hadn't been when he lied to the entire organization about this event.

"God and Mary help us," he groused, then took a deep breath and walked toward his bedroom. He paused when he saw Morgan lying on the bed, as still and pale as a piece of Irish china. Her color would come back when she drank some of the blood stored in the small bedroom refrigerator. At least someone, presumably Danielle, had taken the awful hospital gown off her and dressed her in a soft, burgundy-colored robe.

He sat on the side of the bed and slid his hand beneath Morgan's neck, and noticed her left hand lifted slightly. That was a sign that she'd soon awaken. When he got up to pour blood in two wine glasses, he heard her moan.

He immediately placed the glasses on the small nightstand and sat beside her. He watched her eyelids slowly open and swallowed hard when he gazed down into the most shockingly deep green eyes he'd ever seen. Even vampirism couldn't have induced the striking color.

***

Morgan blinked and tried to focus, but nothing seemed right. She heard what she took to be the sound of an engine and felt movement. When her vision finally began to clear, she barely made out the figure of a man sitting next to her.

He leaned closer.

"Don't try to talk just yet. Take your time."

She stared as his features filtered in and out of focus and noted how the deep timbre of his voice still resonated around her. After a while, her vision adjusted, and she saw his face quite clearly.

She was momentarily stupefied into silence.

The man, whoever he was, was simply gorgeous. His beatific countenance…was exactly how she expected an angel might appear. He had a strong square jaw, full lips, and deep blue eyes. Although his tan *didn't* particularly set him into some angelic category, neither did a day's worth of facial stubble. Strangely, he had long dark hair which fell over his shoulders in thick waves. If he wasn't an angel, what kind of doctor had long hair and didn't keep it pulled back? Where was his white coat? Or was she *really* dead and indeed being attended by some heavenly host?

"It's all right, Morgan. Everything will be okay."

"Wh-Who are you?" she whispered.

"I'm a friend of Patrick's. My name is Sean Reilly. I suppose you've figured out we're not in the hospital."

She turned her head to look around, but the surrounding walls and furnishings began to melt dizzily into each other. She lifted one hand as if doing so could steady her vision. "If I'm not in a hospital, then where am I?"

"You're on a private jet, headed for Ireland."

"So it's true?" she whispered. "People of Irish descent really *do* go back to the old country when they die? And angels escort them there." She blinked, tried to analyze her own silly thoughts, and then caught a glimpse of her *angel* smiling. When she tried to rise, he put one arm around her shoulders, helped her into a sitting position, and arranged the pillows behind her.

"I must have missed a day of catechism. Nobody said anything about jets to Ireland when you die," Morgan ridiculously uttered, then recalled his lilting accent. She gazed at him for a long moment before the seriousness of the situation sank in. "I *was* dying."

Sean met her gaze and nodded. "You *were*. Do you remember what happened?"

"I…I was shot. I could feel the bullets…a frickin' drug bust went wrong." She pushed her hair back and tried to think. "I remember being in the hospital. Uncle Pat came and I remember being taken to the operating room."

"That was four days ago. You had to have another operation because they couldn't stop the bleeding," Sean explained. "Do you recall what Patrick said?"

Morgan nodded. "He held my hand and told me some crazy story to take my mind off…I was scared as hell," she softly admitted, then wrapped her arms around her torso.

***

As they had before, Sean's protective instincts kicked in. None of this was her fault. All she'd done was her job. And it had gotten her killed—as medical science defined the term. No matter what his feelings were over the sad ending, this was business. He'd learned long ago to separate personal emotions from his job.

"You're safe now. No one is going to hurt you, and the bullet wounds are healing. All that's over. You'll be able to see your uncle again when he's finished taking care of some business in Los Angeles. It might not be for a few months, though."

Morgan licked her dry lips. "I…I should be dead. There was no way I could have survived what happened. I remember what the paramedics said to the doctors. And what the doctors said right before they wheeled me into the operating room. I'm sure they didn't know I could hear them but I could."

Sean silently cursed the idiots who spoke around anyone who was injured and in shock. He remembered being carried into the makeshift Army hospital, full of bullets. The medics there had said the same things as he lay bleeding to death. They, too, thought he couldn't hear them and their carelessness made him feel like a piece of meat. He'd been as frightened then as Morgan was now; he actually saw her begin to shake. Again he recalled circumstances leading up to both of them becoming vampires were remarkably similar—although that was another lifetime and he was a different man now with a new identity. Morgan's battlefield had been the streets of Los Angeles, and her enemy had been some animal trying to sell drugs. Yet, their fight to rid the world of savages was the same.

When he placed one hand on her shoulder, the woman leaned toward him. Even now he sensed her vampiric instincts were growing. Still, he noted very human emotions in her expression. Fear, disbelief, and absolute shock were all there.

He remembered those same feelings flowing through him, and he wanted to pull her closer and comfort her in an old fashioned, chivalrous way. Recognizing the bond brought on by his having changed her, he fought the desire and got back to the subject.

"Listen to me, Morgan. You said you remembered Patrick speaking to you. Can you tell me anything he said?"

"He kept telling me some stupid story. It was to take my mind off the pain and I knew it," she admitted with a shrug. "I think he must have seen how much I was hurting and I wasn't talking rationally. I cried like a baby. It was like my intestines were being twisted and pulled in five different directions. My uncle was probably scared shitless and would have said anything."

He silently cursed not having questioned Patrick before being called to Los Angeles. Now, he took the proverbial bull by the horns and got down to showing his initiate she was no longer human. "Morgan, I want you to look at your wounds."

"*What?*"

He put his fingers under her chin. "Look at the bullet wounds in your body." He gently spread her arms, stood, and turned around so she could do as he asked with some degree of privacy. When he heard her gasp and utter a curse, Sean slowly turned around and saw her blankly staring into space. She was now standing and her hands were gripping the fabric of her robe; she'd pulled it around her in a cocoon-like fashion. "Your uncle said you wanted to be part of our organization. He told me you'd been informed about us." He carefully continued. "Hours ago, you took your last breath as a human. Patrick wanted to save you any way he could." He saw her slowly focus back on him.

"What's happened to me?" she whispered.

He took a deep breath, stood squarely in front of her and placed his hands on either side of her face. "You're a vampire…like *me*."

She backed away from him. "This isn't real. I'm not dead…and I am *not* a vampire! I'm still breathing. I'm taking air into my lungs."

"That's an autonomic response we never lose. For us, it just isn't necessary. It's a mechanism that evolved thousands of years ago, so that humans around us *see* us breathing. It's a little like chameleons changing colors so they can survive," Sean said as he tried to get her to accept the situation and calm down. The absolute horrified look in her eyes was one of the most poignant things he'd ever witnessed. He now understood the reason for the rules. No one should come to this way of life without knowing what would happen first.

"In the bathroom, there's a mirror. It's only there for my assistant's benefit. I don't need it. Go take a look."

Morgan stumbled toward the small room. When she threw open the door and saw *nothing* in the mirror, her legs folded. He moved forward to catch her before she hit the floor. She wouldn't have been hurt if she had, but he still acted out of instinct. Having nowhere else to put her, he deposited her on the bed again.

For a time, he waited for her response and tried to figure out their next move. "I'll let you talk to your uncle if it'll make you feel better."

Morgan nodded.

Sean retrieved a cell phone from a cabinet. To make sure only Patrick was contacted, he dialed the memorized number for her. He then handed her the phone when it made the connection.

To give her some distance, he walked into the next room but not so far that he couldn't quickly intervene if she attempted another call.

In this instance, he reasoned that allowing Morgan to

make her short contact hardly mattered considering the breach of operating procedure Patrick had already engaged.

Normally, it was a serious violation to phone any operative, human or vampire, in the field. Doing so could compromise their wellbeing. Though Morgan's uncle was technically retired, he could be considered on duty and *in the field* in this instance. Patrick had called in this initiation because policy permitted him latitude in doing so. But his actions made him responsible for tying up loose ends in Los Angeles.

Procedure stated agents could only use cell phones or the internet in dire emergencies, or to report in when they safely could. Even then, the conversations were brief and coded. It was feared the theft or misplacement of such devices and any information therein, could cause the agency a lot of trouble. Strict adherence to the rules governing their use was mandatory. Again, he could see no harm in allowing Morgan her phone time. This was a minor indiscretion compared to

Patrick's actions. If the call would help calm Morgan, then so be it.

While in the main cabin and still a cautious few feet from where Morgan conversed with her uncle, he poured himself a glass of blood from the bar. That was when he remembered Morgan hadn't had any. She would need it soon and he was pretty sure the offer wasn't going to make the situation any better.

He'd finished his third drink and was rinsing out his glass when she walked into the larger cabin area which also served as his office.

Morgan handed the phone back to him.

He decided to slide it into a dump bin connected to the next cabin. Dani would retrieve it and keep it with her gear. If Morgan noted the extra bit of security, she said nothing. In fact, she seemed a bit confused or distracted.

"My uncle told me that he couldn't talk on the phone about...*certain things*. He said not to call him again, and I should get you to explain," she absently relayed.

Sean rolled his eyes, sighed, and sat down in a nearby chair. It was a bit too late for Patrick to start following the rules. So, *he* would be stuck with answering Morgan's questions. "Ask anything you like."

She wrapped her robe tighter around her body and spoke slowly. "Let's start over, okay?" Then she paced for a moment before saying, "I don't remember a lot of what my uncle told me. It sounded like a load of crap!"

Sean waved a hand at the upholstered seat opposite him. When she sat down, he started with the most logical explanation—the truth. "The name of our organization is *The Nightwatchers*. It was secretly formed hundreds of years ago, as a way for conscionable vampires to co-exist with mankind. We use our powers to ferret out certain criminal elements that the law in most countries can't touch. In this day and age, you might call us the world's largest and most elite anti-terrorist unit."

He waited for some response, but she only stared back—apparently waiting for him to continue. The actual history of the organization was more complicated, but he'd settle for what she might currently accept and leave the specifics for another time.

"Support for what we do comes from some eighty countries," he explained, "but only necessary government officials know who we are and what we do. Human and vampire operatives handle everything from field ops to surveillance and more. As with the majority of humans," he relayed, "not even most vampires know the agency exists. Those chosen to join us swear an oath to keep the organization secret. As I've implied, only those with a need to know are briefed. We're as far above any governmental law enforcement agencies as the sky is above the ocean floor." Once again, he waited for a response and finally got one.

"*Conscionable* vampires, huh?"

"That's right. We're not all the blood-sucking monsters

Hollywood depicts. No more than humans are all warmongering, horrifying sociopaths. Most of us have a need to live in a peaceful world. We try to make that happen."

She watched him closely, as if she were trying to decide whether he was crazy or *she* was.

"I never knew my uncle had anything to do with this...*Nightwatchers*...group. He told me he sold agricultural equipment."

Sean shrugged. "That's as good a cover as any. It would explain why he traveled, especially to parts of the world where his presence might otherwise be questioned. After all, every country on the planet is engaged in agricultural pursuits."

"I guess it was why he was never around before my parents died."

Sean leaned back and tried to relax. As long as she could talk coherently, they could find a solution to this predicament. In fact, she was taking things much better than he'd anticipated. "Pat officially retired from the organization when your parents were killed…an airplane crash wasn't it?"

She nodded.

"Since he was your only relation, he was allowed to leave us to see to your upbringing; but only as long as he checked in regularly."

"You seem to know a lot about my history. But then I guess you *would* if you're some kind of covert agent."

He was more than just an agent, but his exact position could be explained later. "Your uncle advised us that he'd begun a recruitment process with you. It normally starts as a scenario where the recruit is given a series of hypothetical questions about their political beliefs and their opinions regarding law enforcement. Those eventually chosen to undergo recruitment have proven themselves trustworthy and are loyal to certain causes. Suffice it to say, we've never approached anyone we *didn't* believe would eventually join us," he explained and then paused to let his words sink in before continuing. "The individuals we employ are people who crave this lifestyle. They desire a sense of purpose and fulfillment that comes with serving democracy. They're freedom lovers. It might take time for the process to culminate in the recruit being hired but, as I said, we don't approach those with beliefs other than our own. To do so wouldn't be prudent, as I'm sure you understand."

Morgan nodded. "My Uncle Pat has all those qualities. I often wondered why he never became a cop."

"He was in our organization for almost twenty years when he left to take care of you. And he never violated any procedure…until *now*," Sean added. "He let us believe he was in the process of recruiting you and that you were agreeable to following our regulations as a *human* member of the organization. When you were shot and dying, Pat asked for me to initiate you into vampirism. He said you agreed to this, knowing what would be expected of you."

She leaned forward. "How much trouble is he in? And

don't screw with me either!"

Straight from the hip. Sean had to give her points for knowing that what Patrick had done could have very serious consequences. "Let's just say no one has ever done what he has. If our supervisors find out you never agreed to this and that you weren't ever properly briefed and recruited as your uncle claimed, I don't hold much chance for his survival."

"You'd kill him? Just like that?" she angrily asked.

Sean noted the outrage in her voice but it couldn't be helped. "What do you think a member of your country's CIA would do with an operative who compromised the safety of his fellow agents? A great many people went to huge expense to falsify documents and evolve a cover story to get you on this jet. All it would take to unravel everything is if you returned to Los Angeles, not only alive but completely healthy."

"How did you get me out of the hospital and bypass a required autopsy? Somebody has to be asking questions," she demanded.

Sean slowly shook his head. "As in most major cities of the world, our people work in very high-ranking, necessary positions. For example, there was a doctor at your hospital who's a member of *Nightwatchers*. He and others are on our payroll even though they only respond to directives when needed. You can see how beneficial this would be if one of our human agents needed medical help and we didn't want questions asked. But just like many of them don't know who I am, I don't know all of them by name. Sharing identities would compromise our collective safety. The less we all know, the less we can say if forced to answer questions. It's very much like you going undercover and not letting the entire police force know you're doing so. Understand?"

She swallowed hard. "The kind of cooperative effort you're talking about would be massive. Are you saying you *literally* walked into a hospital several days after I was shot and commandeered everything? Newspaper reporters would want to know about the shooting. The medical examiner would want my autopsy for evidence in a trial. There would be judges, lawyers, politicians, and police officials to deal with. Not to mention friends who'd be asking questions. I don't understand how you could just take me and get away with it."

"I understand you were involved in an undercover operation when you were shot."

"Yeah…so?"

"All we had to do was plant a story that you were secretly working for a much bigger, more covert agency. We might even let the local authorities infer it was the CIA. It's probably being said your pursuit of drug dealers was directly related to terrorist group funding. Drug money *does* fund terrorists, after all. And when the story is couched that way, all kinds of officials would bend over backwards to make sure we got any help we needed. And there are very important people at the top levels of your government, who would make sure *no one* got in our way." He paused. "As for the autopsy and all the rest, the paperwork will be filed, and the authorities will be told we're handling the case from here on. Your friends will be told your body was cremated. There'll be a nice memorial service, and you'll be perceived as another statistic in an on-going war against terrorism."

"You said we're headed to Ireland. *Why*?"

"You have to go somewhere where you can lay low. Since Patrick got me into this, I see no reason to take you anyplace but back with me. For now, Ireland is my center of operation and I need to resume duties." He finally saw where her solicitous and extraordinary acceptance of the situation was leading. The woman had been questioning him in an effort to find out what she *really* thought was happening. Her growing anger was now revealing her caginess.

"Listen…*ace*," she addressed him caustically, "I'm not a…a *'statistic'* as you put it. And what the hell makes you think I'd join?"

Sean raised one brow. "You'd better consider it. It would solve a lot of problems."

"Why should I? I mean, why bother *asking*? No one has so far," she retorted.

He held his misgivings at bay and tried to stay on her rational, less angry side. "I'm sorry for my part in this, Morgan. Your uncle wasn't at the hospital when I got there, or I'd have probably seen right through his deception. Though it happens, it isn't easy for a human to lie to one of us. Our senses, as you'll soon discover, are usually keener than any mortal's. But I still take responsibility for not checking out Pat's story. I trusted him. We've known each other for a long time, and I would never have believed him capable of a shenanigan like this. But the result is that he saved you from the grave and gave you a chance at continuing a useful, fulfilling existence."

"I'd have liked to have made the decision myself," she angrily insisted. "He could have done exactly as you've explained. He could have approached me as a recruit. Now...*you* say I'm a damned vampire without a clue as to what I'm doing."

He leaned forward and stared into her green eyes. "You *are* a vampire," he stated. "It shouldn't have happened, but it's done and can't be changed. There's no cure for it that we know of. And maybe Pat actually meant to recruit you sooner or later; he didn't have time to consider that course after you were shot. Though I shouldn't be defending his actions, your uncle is only human. He panicked and did what he thought was best. Still, even if it was wrong, you were a police officer. A damned good one from all accounts," Sean placated. "Why would you be willing to die for what you believe, and not want to live now for those same convictions? It makes no sense."

He sensed her absolute frustration and saw both anger and fear in her face. She stood and turned away from him for a moment. When she turned back around, there was a determined look on her face, and he couldn't help being drawn to the assertive flash in those striking green eyes.

"If I try this and don't like it, can I leave?" she asked.

Sean stood and moved to within a foot of her. "Will you swear, on your life and that of your uncle's, that you'll never compromise this organization or its members?"

She nodded. "Whatever it takes."

Sean believed her. For that particular moment in time, there was no deception in the way she said it or in her expression. "Then I'll plan for you to safely leave. Until *then,* you have to convince everyone we contact that you're with me of your own free will."

"And if I can't?"

"If my superiors find out about this, your uncle just might become one of those people who mysteriously disappear off the face of the Earth," Sean offered. "I can only imagine what will happen to *you*. Being shot to death might seem like a walk in the park compared to how a vampire is hunted down and destroyed."

"Is that a threat?" She lifted her chin and stared straight into his eyes. "Is this the behavior of a so-called peace loving, democratic crime fighting organization?"

"Call it a warning. The same way the members of *The Nightwatchers* will bend over backwards to save one of their operatives in trouble, they'll go after anyone who compromises the organization's safety. Let's not test the waters, shall we?"

Chapter 2

She watched him walk into the small bedroom. With every moment that passed, Morgan wanted to be farther from this nightmare. She'd play this silly part until those around her were convinced she just wouldn't make a good operative. Acting like she was in on the deal would get Pat off the hook. And when he was safe and she knew she could make her escape, Sean Reilly and his precious *Nightwatchers* organization could kiss her ass. He'd probably chosen to be what he was. She hadn't. She was no one's *statistic*.

When Sean returned, he was holding what looked like a glass of wine. She wasn't fooled. "Is that what I think it is?"

Sean nodded. "It's better at room temperature. I meant to have you drink it when you first woke up."

She pointed at the glass. "I'm not drinking that. Who did you slaughter to get it or what animal got mutilated?" she viciously asked.

He frowned and sat the glass in front of her. "I don't harm animals. The blood comes from human volunteers. Most vampires don't kill people anymore. It draws too much attention. Those of our world who are independents prefer to steal their next meal from blood banks or other sources. Like I said, the vampires in *Nightwatchers* are lucky enough to have our human agents volunteer the blood."

"I don't care…I'm not drinking it." She crossed her arms over her chest and tossed her hair back.

Sean sat in front of her. "Sooner or later, you're going to have to. I've mixed it with a little wine to make it more palatable. Eventually, you won't need or want the wine. We don't eat or drink anything else."

Morgan simply stared at him.

"Maybe I'd better explain a few other things about our kind," he offered. "I'm not sure you even fully believe you are what you've been changed into, so let me make it crystal clear."

"It's not like I'm goin' anywhere," she furiously returned as she gestured at her surroundings.

He ignored her and continued. "We can be killed by sunlight, decapitation, a wooden or silver stake through the heart…and fire. Pretty much everything legend has listed with a few exceptions as follows: though we don't eat food, being around garlic doesn't bother us; we don't need to be invited into any structure to gain access. We can actually hold silver for a little while, without being burned, but when our bodies are pierced by it we can be hurt very badly…as I've already mentioned. Crosses don't bother us in the least nor does holy water. I carry a crystal crucifix and accept communion from a *Nightwatchers* priest. It follows that entering churches has no adverse effect whatsoever."

When she failed to respond, he continued. "There *are* those of us who are known as *ancients*. They're much older and have evolved powers that're substantial. They can exist in limited light and can actually take in food. If you ever run into one, you'll sense their powers are unique. I'll tell you more about them sometime, but for now it's enough that you realize our blood—mine *and* yours—is wholly vampire. For us, *almost* all the old legendary clichés apply regarding our powers. So you'll have to get used to the situation, Morgan. I don't like having changed someone against their will. I've already apologized and won't do it again. This is your life now. I suggest you deal with it!"

"Deal with *what*?" she vehemently responded. "I'm not alive anymore, I'm dead. What's there to deal with?"

"And reality finally begins to set in," he quipped as he briefly closed his eyes. "This is what I was afraid of."

Morgan glared at him and pointed at the glass full of blood. "What happens if I don't drink it?"

"You'll wish you had."

She moved to a chair across the aisle, picked up a magazine and did her best to ignore him.

"Morgan—"

"Go to hell!"

Sean let out a frustrated sigh. "Fine. Do as you please. When the sun comes up, we'll be landing to refuel. You'll feel the need to sleep. If you haven't taken blood by then, you're going to find yourself very ill by the time you awaken. Those newly changed need a lot of nourishment," he instructed.

Morgan patently ignored him and continued to read the magazine. This was obviously all some kind of perverse setup. She'd never really believed she was a damned vampire in the first place. Her mind kept considering how he'd rigged the mirror *not* to reflect an image, but it was obviously doable. What *wasn't* doable any longer was her continued role in this charade. She'd played long enough; there was no reason to humor him anymore. Everything he'd said was impossible. Her rage grew exponentially because he didn't even *try* to act convincing.

Somebody believed she was so stupid that this little performance would fly. Even her healed wounds could be explained if she'd been unconscious for *weeks* instead of days, and some kind of cosmetic surgery had been applied to remove the scars. The only concern now was why anyone would go to this much trouble. She owned nothing of value and no one paid ransom for cops. So, what could this man possibly want?

"Are you listening to me, Morgan?"

Through with games and acting imbecilic to try and draw out answers, she shot him her middle finger. Infantile as the gesture was, it made her feel better and the resulting look of anger on his face was worth it.

"Why did Patrick put himself in shaggin' danger by going to the trouble?" He dragged a hand through his hair in frustration. "Since you're so determined to play the martyr, you can sleep on the sofa. I'll take the bedroom. You can use the shower if you like. I'll leave your luggage in the hall outside the bedroom door. Don't disturb me. I'm not used to having anyone near. If you wake me too early, I won't answer for the consequences."

Morgan watched him pick up a briefcase and walk to the back part of the airplane. She would cut out her tongue before admitting that her stomach was already beginning to ache. A delayed reaction to a drug might explain the queasiness. She wasn't prone to anxiety attacks but wouldn't dismiss her growing physical discomfort as just that under the circumstances. Maybe she was even suffering the effects of an ulcer. But vampirism? No. There were no such things as vampires. Before she'd fall for a load of shit, she'd get to the bottom of why she was on board a plane headed for Ireland, *if* that's where they even were flying.

After she was sure he wasn't coming back, she wandered around the cabin looking at the equipment and poking into things. There was no sign of who the man really was—no papers or documentation of any kind. She decided that, in the way of luxury, there wasn't much the aircraft didn't include. It looked as if it was designed for its arrogant con artist.

Black leather covered the chairs and large sofa. The carpet and walls were a light cream hue. There were no windows, and she couldn't find any sign of an emergency exit. The door to the front of the plane was secured from the inside. Common sense told her not to open it. She tried to convince herself the reason for doing so wasn't because sunlight might get in. Rather, she rationalized there might be someone on the other side that she didn't want to encounter.

On the ground was a better place to handle any dangerous situation, not thousands of feet in the air. She turned and continued to inspect the cabin area in hopes of finding anything that could tell her what was going on. She noted every detail, including the fact that the built-in desk and computer were the best money could buy. She attempted to access the internet but couldn't get by a password initiator. From her inspection, Morgan surmised her tormentor must do pretty damned well for himself, or this *pretend Nightwatchers* organization didn't spare any expense when it came to its *imaginary* operatives' comfort. On a police detective's salary, she'd never have been able to afford a ticket in the baggage compartment of this aircraft, much less have restricted access to the cabin.

Sometime later, the pain in her stomach began to grow and radiate to every other part of her body. She glanced at the glass of blood and immediately recoiled. To keep from even considering this option, she poured the red stuff down the drain in the cocktail bar. For all she knew, it could be drugged. This would explain the need for more. If she were suffering some kind of withdrawal, a drug in the drink would be the only way to counteract her symptoms…or make them worse.

As time went on, her pain became severe and dizziness forced her onto the sofa. She stretched out and tried to think about something else. Her earlier inspection of the cabinets revealed no medical supplies of any kind, not even aspirin. But what could aspirin do for her? If she'd been given a drug with a delayed effect, aspirin could make the situation worse. So she decided to just tough it out and wait. Above all, she had to try and get calmly through this. She was no quitter and wouldn't submit to hysterics. Whatever was going on, Pat was in on it.

She knew her beloved uncle wouldn't do anything to hurt her, however, he *would* make a deal with the devil himself if he thought her life was in jeopardy. Still, Morgan refused to consider her dark companion's explanation. She was *not* a vampire.

***

Sean finished the last of the documents Danielle had prepared for him. He put the paperwork back in his briefcase, showered, and changed into his robe. He sensed the plane was slowing and would probably land to refuel soon. Curious as to why Morgan was so quiet and why she hadn't availed herself of the television or sound system, he opened the bedroom door and glanced around the cabin. When he couldn't immediately see her, he walked forward. "Dammit, Morgan! I tried to tell you." She lay curled into a fetal position, clutching her upper arms, and shaking violently. Her eyes were closed, but he knew she could hear him. Refusal to take blood always presented with these symptoms. "All right, my girl. If I have to pour the blood down your obstinate little throat, then that's the way it'll be."

Sean turned his back on her and walked into his bedroom. He poured a glass of fresh blood from the small supply in his refrigerator then walked back into the cabin. He slid his arm around her shoulders.

Morgan turned her head away, but he put the glass to her lips. "Drink it," he commanded.

Morgan slapped the glass away. It flew across the cabin, struck the opposite wall, and shattered. The red, sticky, substance dripped down the creamy wall and onto the once pristine carpet.

"You little…you'll damned well drink the blood or I'll

sit on you and force it down," he promised as he filled another glass and sat next to her.

He put one hand on her shoulder to steady her shaking, then held the glass close to her nostrils. As was always the case with the newly changed, who clung to their human revulsion of the substance, the smell of the blood finally lured her.

Morgan finally opened her mouth and let him pour her a sip of the dark red liquid through her lips.

He gave an inward sigh of relief. As soon as the taste of it was on her tongue, he didn't need to urge. She gripped the glass with both hands and immediately drank it down.

"The pain and dizziness should fade now," he triumphantly advised, but then regretted his attitude when Morgan leaned forward and stared at her empty glass. He almost felt the disgust she experienced and momentarily commiserated when she tried to cover her embarrassment by not looking at him.

Instead of pushing his coup, he got up, refilled her glass once more and then sat beside her. "It's all right, Morgan. I had the same response the first time I drank blood. I knew I had to but I still fought the urge…same as you." And he wondered why he even admitted such a thing to her when he hadn't ever done so to any other being.

He sensed she was trying hard to act strong. For someone used to being in control of a situation—someone like a police officer—having that power taken away from you was one of the most difficult things in the world. But she had to trust him or none of this was going to work. "No one expects this to come easy for you. But think of all the good you could do, Morgan. Think of all the people you could help."

"While watching every human around me die of old age, suffer sickness, and live perfectly normal lives? Isn't that part of what happens with…*vampires*?" She glibly responded while staring at the glass of blood for a brief moment. She then slowly took it from his hand.

"All this is true. You won't ever be able to have children or live as a human. But I'll show you a few things that might balance the loss. Just try not to fight this so much. You'll make it harder than it needs to be," he recommended.

He watched her briefly close her eyes, raise the glass to her lips and swallow a good mouthful of the liquid. The nourishment would yield strength and clarity. Without thinking, he lifted his hand to touch her long hair but quickly pulled it back when the landing gear was suddenly lowered. That meant it would be sunlight soon. "You'll feel the desire to sleep. Don't fight it."

"We don't sleep in coffins or on soil taken from our homeland? Isn't that what vampires are supposed to do?" she sarcastically asked.

He ignored the mocking question. "That's another of the untrue legends. There are some vampires who sleep on home earth, in coffins. It makes them feel psychologically better...*somehow*. All you need to do is to lean back and try to rest. Let the blood do its job."

Morgan leaned back, closed her eyes and remained quiet. A few moments later, they landed. He heard the plane being refueled.

As soon as they were ready to take off, as indicated by a light on a forward panel, he saw her visibly relax. Her entire body seemed to slump, and he took her glass so it wouldn't fall on the floor as her long, graceful fingers extended.

"Time to rest now. Don't worry, Morgan, things won't be as bad as you might imagine." He watched her half-turn into the sofa and felt the pull of the sun himself. Being a much older vampire, he could hold out just a bit longer and now took the opportunity to stare at her as she relaxed. "Rest, lass. I promise it'll be all right. I won't let anything happen to you," he softly said, although he knew she was far too lost in sleep to hear.

Then, as the sunlight outside the plane pushed him toward the darkness of vampiric sleep, he imagined an entirely different situation existed—one where he could have a relationship with someone who shared some of the same beliefs. From the profile Patrick had provided, he knew that he and Morgan had a great many ideals in common, including their independent natures.

One thing they *didn't* share was their motivation. Becoming what he was had been his choice, albeit after being mortally wounded. He hoped she could eventually come to terms with what had been done to her. If not, the consequences could be deadly serious. Pat would certainly be put to death.

Since this was a probable outcome of this situation, he'd outwardly reacted to her proximity as if he didn't really care. It was a defense mechanism. Over the years, he'd learned never to get too close to anyone. Still, while she slept he could enjoy an imaginary state where possibilities existed.

She was so damned beautiful, so soft and sensual. He could, for the moment, let his guard drop and enjoy her beguiling presence. When she woke again, he could slip the mask of control back on and no one would be the wiser.

If Morgan *did* choose to join the organization, he decided it would be better for her to work in another part of the world. England or France would be better. Or maybe Africa or someplace far enough away that he wouldn't get word of her activities except by asking. Since he'd be her temporary supervisor in the event she *did* become an agent, getting her out of his life could be arranged.

He ran one hand over his face. Her presence was unnerving. He was feeling too much and attributed this to his having been the one to change her. He knew how to detach those sensations and would. There was no place for emotional upheaval in his life. Morgan Grady was lovely if a tough little package. These were characteristics he'd always found extremely attractive in women.

As he drifted off, his memories harkened back to the war and Simone. It was at rare times like this, when he let emotion overwhelm his rational side, that Simone's presence seemed very near. *She* was the one who entered his dreams…not some changeling named *Morgan Grady.*

***

He awoke on the same sofa where she rested. His reawakening happened just as the plane touched down. Ireland was in his blood, so he knew homeland when he was back on it.

He'd never made it to the bedroom. And now he looked at Morgan's face and, despite his intent to detach, felt the sudden desire to hold her. In her deathlike sleep, she'd somehow managed to throw one slender thigh over his lap. Her robe had opened and he got a very tempting look at her long, shapely leg. The inside of her thigh was almost touching his groin. Her soft body caused him to respond the way any man would. Carefully, disengaging himself from her slumbering form, he immediately walked into the bedroom and tried to regain control.

When Patrick was finished in Los Angeles, the man was going to answer for a hell of a lot. In the very brief time he'd known her, Morgan was becoming a complication and not just because she'd been changed without her permission. Dragging both hands through his hair, he didn't understand why he couldn't simply disconnect from her as he would from any other initiate.

The buzzing of the intercom startled him. He quickly hit the wall button. "Yes?"

"We'll be able to open the outer hatch in a few moments, Sean. How's Morgan doing? Would you like me to come back there?" Danielle asked.

"I think that would be best, Dani," he ordered, while using the more common, shortened version of his assistant's name. "She isn't awake yet but might accept a woman's help better than mine."

"Of course. And we should get back to Greenwood as soon as possible. There's been some communication you'll need to deal with."

"Anything serious?"

Dani's silence answered his question.

"Have Thomas relieved and tell him to take the next two days off."

"Will do," Dani replied. "The driver's already arrived with the car from Greenwood. I called ahead. There should be a room ready for Morgan as well."

He smiled. "Thanks, Dani. What would I do without you?"

"Flounder helplessly I should imagine."

Sean was about to shoot back a sarcastic reply when he heard the ground crew readying the exit ramp outside the plane. "I'd better check on our *guest*. I'll unlock the door and let you into the main cabin."

He clicked the intercom off and walked back into the lounge area. Morgan was sitting up and pushing her beautiful hair back with one hand. She looked at him, and her expression had a kind of *what now* wistfulness he found hard to resist. He steeled himself to do just that.

"You might want to get dressed. We've landed and a driver is waiting to take us to our safe house."

"Where exactly are we?" she asked as she slowly stood.

"Dublin. It'll take us about an hour to make the final leg of the trip. There's someone in the outer cabin who'll answer any questions. Her name is Danielle Fraser. She's my personal assistant, and I expect you to seriously heed any advice she gives as well as any of my instructions."

"Is she a vampire?"

"No. Dani is human as are the other people who comprise my staff. You should be able to tell she isn't one of us as soon as I let her in the cabin." He walked to the main door separating the two parts of the plane and unlocked it. "Normally, Dani stays with me during long flights, but I thought it might be better to have some privacy given the circumstances. As it happens, it was a wise decision. It gave you a little time to work through some of the juvenile, irrational behavior you've displayed," he said with more austerity than was necessary. "Dani is far too busy to be inflicted with your problems right now. Nor should she have to take the brunt of your anger."

When Sean turned and saw the fury in her green gaze, he was almost glad. His insult had worked.

This was the way it had to be. This was no life for people who became too emotionally attached. And if she found his behavior unacceptable, it would make it much easier for *him* to withstand her presence; much less likely they would ever get close.

***

Morgan immediately took her gaze off Sean and put it on the cabin door as it opened. A tall, strawberry blonde walked in. Despite her being somewhere in her fifties, she was an exquisite-looking woman. Her hair was pinned in a neat French bun, and her tweed suit fit her slender figure perfectly.

Morgan felt relief when the woman openly smiled and walked forward with her arms wide. There was a definite difference between this woman and Sean. An air of vulnerability clung to Danielle. Morgan felt physically stronger in every way, but she chalked it up to being younger and in good *human* health.

"Hello, Morgan. Patrick has told me so much about you. I know you already," Dani greeted.

Morgan accepted her hug. "How do you know my uncle?"

"I'm his contact in the organization. Once one of our operatives leaves the agency, they're supposed to stay connected or our agents go looking for them. It's just a way to keep them safe and–"

"I think I've enlightened Morgan enough about her uncle's part in the agency," Sean broke into Dani's explanation. "Can you make sure Morgan gets into some clothes and out to the limo? I want to get back to Greenwood as soon as possible. I've wasted enough time on this chicanery."

"Of course," Dani agreed while staring pointedly at her employer.

Sean put Morgan's luggage in the cabin, then turned and walked toward the bathroom.

Morgan waited for him to be out of earshot. She needed to get Dani alone and off guard. Only then could she get some answers. Something told her the older woman might slip and give information away.

"I can't imagine how horrifying this whole ordeal must be for you," Dani said as she put an arm around Morgan's shoulders. "But I'll help in any way I can. If you need anything at all, no matter how late at night, you can come to me."

Morgan was momentarily taken aback. The older woman's voice, with its cultured English accent, sounded completely sincere. It was hard to understand why Sean's assistant would act so instantly warm. But maybe this was all part of the grand scheme—just one more way to get under her skin. She simply nodded her thanks for the offer and smiled at the lovely woman. "I'll get dressed," Morgan announced pleasantly and opened a suitcase that the older woman provided for her.

Danielle stood to one side and helped pick some things for her to wear.

She watched Dani's face closely as the older woman sorted clothing. "Someone did an excellent job of packing my belongings. But I'm afraid they could have left my makeup kit behind. I can't put it on without a mirror. And since I can't see my reflection…" Morgan stopped and waited for the comment to provoke a telltale guilty response, but the older woman didn't even wince. If Dani was in on this part of the scheme, she exhibited no outward sign.

"I'll be your mirror," Dani sweetly offered. "Just give me the makeup and I'll put it on for you. Just put yourself in my hands, my dear. I'm a veritable wizard and stay on top of all the trends where makeup and clothing are concerned."

"That's very kind of you." There was no logical reason for Danielle to be nice. Morgan didn't accept for a moment that she could trust this woman any more than she could Sean. Probably even their names were aliases.

"You've a lovely face, dear. You're one of those lucky women who doesn't even need makeup, though a little touch here and there gives us women confidence, doesn't it?" Dani asked, as she worked. "Just remember, Morgan…you're among friends and it's all right to ask questions. I know this is terribly ill done of us. Your Uncle Patrick is a good man, but he should never have put you through this," she asserted. "He should have told you who we were and about this part of his life a long time ago. I can only assume he didn't try to recruit you earlier because he didn't know how to explain this agency. He told me how much you loved your work. Perhaps he thought you'd never want to leave it…especially since you were such a good police officer."

“Obviously not good enough,” Morgan pointed out as she pulled her jeans on. “I went and got myself shot.”

“And now you have the chance to keep the same thing from happening to a lot of other people, dear. Indirectly, some other police officer might go home to his or her family because you could help.”

Morgan stopped dressing for a moment. This was a strange comment coming from someone she considered a captor.

“Finish dressing and I’ll fix your hair. From here on out, you’ve got the chance to change the world, Morgan. So few women ever get the opportunities you will. The men in this organization won’t know what hit them when you get your feet under you and become acquainted with your powers. I have a feeling you’re going to be absolutely smashing,” Dani praised.

Something in the older woman’s kind smile and soft voice tempted Morgan, but she silently steeled herself not to fall for this innovative approach. Here was someone who was pretending to give a damn about her. It was the old *I'm someone you can relate to* routine. Instead of trusting Dani as the older woman obviously wanted, Morgan simply smiled and bided her time. She wasn't nearly as gullible as these people assumed. In fact, Danielle could be the weak point in this entire show. The older woman was someone who might just slip up and reveal what the hell was really going on.

***

Morgan sat inside the limousine, watched the driver take Sean's bag, and place it in the trunk. Danielle was on her cell phone, speaking with one of the staff at a place called Greenwood. This was, apparently, where they were taking her.

She stared out the window as Sean got in and sat across from Danielle. He didn't acknowledge her presence, nor did she care.

As soon as Dani put the phone down, her two captors

began to converse with each other. Morgan kept her mouth closed, and her eyes on the darkened hillsides, as they left the city lights behind. She had to get her bearings and figure out how to get back to the city, from wherever this Greenwood place was.

One thing puzzled her. No landing crew or security officers approached the aircraft or the limousine after they landed. When curiosity finally overwhelmed her, she broke into a lull in the mundane conversation between Sean and Danielle.

"Why weren't we subjected to any security when we landed? We'd have been in a hell of a fix if someone had stopped us. I assume I don't have any identification."

Danielle closed her leather organizer and smiled at Morgan. "I'll take care of it when we're back at Greenwood. A fake passport and anything else will be provided. I'll use your police photos, carefully computer altered and enhanced of course, on your new identification. For the time being, you can keep your first name, as it's familiar to you. But we'll have to find another surname. As for leaving the airport so easily, security here has been given strict orders not to stop us under any circumstances," Danielle explained.

Morgan was alarmed by the answer, but she asked what she assumed would be the proper question in this situation. "Isn't all this subterfuge risky? Seems like it would attract less attention if you tried to blend in and act like anyone else arriving on a private flight."

Danielle nodded. "It would seem so. But there are rules all Allied countries have mutually agreed to, regarding our arriving and leaving their airports. Of course, only a handful of individuals in these countries actually know who we are. Mostly, the local police and the military are led to believe we're on crucial political business. A higher state of diplomatic immunity applies. When you're working in a world where terrorists can cause such horrifying destruction, we have to be able to come and go expeditiously. Those countries allowing us to do so enjoy the benefits of our protection. They don't question anything, but simply accept what we do."

Morgan leaned back in the soft leather seat and considered again the power that this pretend organization called *Nightwatchers,* or its officials, must have at their disposal. Either they really *could* do anything they wanted or she was being lied to on a scale unwarranted given her lack of importance in the world. If the first situation were true…this kind of power could be devastating.

She was only *somewhat* mollified by the realization that her own country's highly placed officials were among those being conned by these people. What happened to *her* couldn't have taken place otherwise. It seemed she wasn't the only dupe in this scheme.

Evidently, the fake identification Danielle referred to was only constructed so they could travel in areas away from airports and where they had no control. Morgan was besieged by old movie images where spies used gadgets and disguises to complete missions.

But why the vampire routine? What probable reason could anyone have for letting her believe such things existed and that she was one of them? This entire scheme was absurd. There was no doubt her captors' power were considerable. But power didn't impress her. She meant to get to the bottom of this entire insane plot.

"Is something wrong?"

Since the question came from Sean, Morgan decided to just shake her head in response and kept her gaze on the passing scenery. There was no sense getting into any discussion with him. Not when Danielle might be induced to answer questions later. No, let them think they had her right where they wanted her.

When Dani and Sean began to converse once again, she pretended to ignore every word. Even in the darkness outside the expensive limo, it seemed that she could make out details;

details that shouldn't have been visible given the darkness. She again wondered if the drugs were altering her eyesight she'd been given. As to the rest of her health, she had none of the sickness which plagued her before drinking the blood…and it *was* blood she drank though likely mixed with some illicit substance. This fact was indisputable. It was what was *in* it that had her concerned.

"Morgan?"

Dani's tap on her shoulder brought her back into reality. Sean was offering *her* a wine glass filled with blood and handing Danielle a diet soda at the same time. She took the offering, nodded her thanks and pretended to drink. Her lips went to the edge of the glass, but she didn't swallow. Angry he'd try giving her drugged-laced blood again, she didn't feel like communicating with him. She believed there was something in the concoction making her want it more. There was no other reason for her desperately craving another sip of the foul stuff.

"Uh, surely you'd like to ask us something about Ireland or where we're headed?" Danielle asked in an attempt to get Morgan to speak.

"I know it's called Greenwood. Beyond that, if our positions were reversed, I wouldn't tell me anything. You don't really know who I am and what I might do. Just because I was a cop in Los Angeles doesn't mean I'll be an appropriate member of your, uh, *organization*. In fact, I'd be checking me out a lot more thoroughly if I were you."

Morgan hadn't meant to be so bitchy with her answer. Her behavior wouldn't win her points with Danielle, but she disliked being a victim. She just flat didn't feel like saying anything around Sean at all. Her part in any conversation was over for the time being. She quickly turned her attention to the window again.

"Your sudden concern for our security is heartwarming," Sean remarked. "You'll be glad to know we *did* thoroughly check you out, Morgan. We wouldn't have wasted the time, money, or manpower to bring you here otherwise. You and your background aren't the problem. Pat's lie about your being properly recruited *is*."

Morgan simply shot him a cursory glance and kept silent. Again she wondered what her uncle had to do with all this. She had to find out and get word to him. Surely, he didn't know what was being done to her despite Sean's assertion to the contrary. She couldn't bring herself to believe her own kin was agreeable to all this. What her uncle had said on the phone was only to assure her safety. What else could he do if she'd been kidnapped? She refused to let Sean bait her and pretended to have more interest in what was outside the limo than the conversation inside.

***

It was over an hour later when the limousine drove up to a set of high, wrought iron gates. Morgan noted the stone wall surrounding this particular piece of property was equally high and imposing. She hardly saw the need for any such barrier if these so-called vampires could do what legend purported.

Why secure the place if they were so damned powerful? If she asked, would Sean simply explain the wall away by saying it existed for the safety of their human counterparts? She was sure he'd produced *some* reason for such a protected compound.

"As you can see, this place is quite isolated," Sean remarked. "The wall keeps local shepherds and farmers from wandering onto our property. It tells them we aren't exactly sociable and don't tolerate trespassers. This house has been one of our properties for generations, though the vampire occupants move on after a while. It wouldn't do to be seen in one place for any length of time and not alter our appearance. Failure to age would certainly cause attention. After a few generations go by, and the current citizens in this area have died off, we can return to those places we once inhabited."

"I'm sure that keeping friendly people away wouldn't

be a problem for *you*," Morgan shot back.

Sean's eyes narrowed.

"W-We have a lovely garden," Dani nervously muttered. "And there's a pond where you can swim at night if you'd like. You'll have a wonderful room that's been sealed against sunlight and a library containing some of the rarest books you can imagine. We have a considerable selection of tunes in our music room and there's even a small dance floor. We have a sauna, workout room, and just about every imaginable amenity."

Morgan noted Dani's rushed words. Partly because she regretted having ignored the older woman's attempts at conversation, and partly because she wanted Sean to know she was still aiming her ire at *him*, Morgan shot Dani the most brilliant smile she could manage. Then, she clasped the older woman's hand in hers as a friendly gesture. "Thanks, Dani. I'm glad to know someone I can *count* on will help me through this."

Morgan didn't miss Sean's cold stare. She simply glared right back.

"Dani, as soon as you're ready, show Ms. Grady to her room. Later, she and I need to discuss household rules," Sean said, instructing his assistant as if Morgan wasn't there and couldn't hear.

Morgan didn't care if Dani responded. She put her attention back on the scenery. The long winding drive didn't prepare her for the building situated behind all the tall trees. A stone castle-like structure loomed ahead. Instead of appearing institutional or cold, its massive presence suddenly warmed her. Her new home was three stories high with a pair of matched cement gryphons on each side of an arched oak doorway. Because her night vision was strangely acute, she saw flowerbeds filled with bright blossoms. "This is beautiful!"

Dani smiled. "There's a lovely garden in back. And several smaller ones situated about the grounds. You really should wander through them in the evening hours. The scent of the flowers alone is marvelous."

Sean echoed Dani's sentiment. "If you feel up to it, why don't you take a walk around the place while we get the luggage inside? Stretch your legs and get used to being in the night. When you're ready, come inside and Dani will show you around, but under no circumstances are you to leave the grounds!"

Morgan wasn't surprised by the sudden warning in his voice. She was, after all, their captive. But the surreptitious nod that passed between the other two led her to believe there was something in the house itself needing care, *before* they wanted her to enter. "Fine. Tell you what. Whenever you're ready, why don't you just get me?" The limo slid to a stop outside the arched door. Morgan quickly got out and ignored the driver's attempts to help her. She gave them all a cursory nod, and then walked toward the expansive, manicured lawn.

***

As soon as Sean was sure Morgan couldn't overhear, he turned to Dani. "Bring me up to date on what's been happening. She's to have no knowledge of any information coming from our superiors."

"But don't you want her to become acquainted with how we operate?"

"I've already told her too much. She's right about my needing to ascertain her capabilities before letting her know more."

"Surely, someone with her background would be able to handle herself. I mean…her file–"

"Her file said she was a good police officer and did excellent undercover work. Ordinarily police work isn't what we're about, as you well know. Furthermore, I want to find out exactly what happened the day she was shot. If her cover was blown, I want to know why. I don't want a repeat of the situation if she *does* decide to stay. She could get someone killed."

Danielle sighed. "Aren't you being a bit harsh?"

He ignored Dani's question about his behavior. "Make doubly sure her room is sealed against the sun and get her when I've had time to re-read her file and make some calls. Then you can brief me on any messages sent while we were flying from the States." He took a deep breath and prepared himself for the inevitable call. As soon as they touched ground at the airport, the pilot should have relayed the landing to his supervisors.

Sean silently prayed they hadn't heard of Patrick's ill-conceived plan to save Morgan. If they had, the old man would die before he ever got to see his niece again.

Chapter 3

Morgan walked into the middle of a wooded area and stopped. The wall looked formidable but she'd had to get past tougher things in life. Being shot was included. And if she could survive five bullets, she could get over the damned barrier. She momentarily considered Pat and what might be happening with him.

As long as she was a captive, for whatever reason, her uncle could be made to do or say anything. If she could make her way back to Dublin, there was a chance to get to the American Embassy and Sean Reilly could deal with the Marine guards there if he chose to show up.

A movement to her left caused Morgan to kneel down in the tall shrubbery and wait. Stealthy, armed guards were patrolling everywhere, but they wouldn't hinder her resolve. All that stood between her and freedom was the damned wall. Somehow, she was determined to get over or under it. And she needed to do it quickly.

The guards stopped for a moment to converse, and she waited for them to move in their separate directions again. As the sound of their departure drifted away, she crept forward. At the foot of the rock wall, she noticed how the stones had been piled upon one another and plastered together. The lights from the compound didn't illuminate this part of the garden particularly well, but it seemed her vision wasn't at all hampered by that fact. She mentally shook off the creepiness instilled by Sean's description of vampiric powers. Her vision was normal for any human. There was no need to let her imagination get the better of her.

All she needed to worry about were the spaces between the rocks providing foot and hand holds. She also needed to watch for the damned guards.

"Hell, better dead than captured," she whispered to herself. "Here goes nothin'." She stood, faced the wall, and began to pull herself straight up the side. It was so much easier than she'd have believed possible…and oddly much quicker. But adrenaline could do wonders for a person.

She was on top of, over and descending the other side of the wall in record time. Thankfully, she'd practiced recreational climbing for years, hence her ability to make short work of this old, plastered structure.

She couldn't help grinning, but her conceited praise in a job well done was short-lived when an alarm went off. One shoulder lifted in a cursory shrug. "Kiss my ass and watch me run!"

She turned and fled into the night, heading in a southerly direction, back toward Dublin. It wouldn't do to get caught out in the open or on a road where her captors would be looking. So, she kept to the scenery and used it to hide her retreat.

***

Inside the large room serving as his office, Sean heard the alarm and stood so fast that the chair he'd been seated in flew backward and flipped over. The double doors opened, and Dani ran into the room.

"It's Morgan—" Dani began.

"Son-of-a…don't tell me! Just let me get my hands on her." He quickly walked past Dani, into the outer hall, through the oak doors leading from the foyer and out into the night. "Wherever you run, you little hellion, I'll find you!"

Knowing Morgan couldn't shapeshift yet, would make her much easier to locate. Sean simply moved forward and hit the wall at a dead run. It took him only a few seconds to scale the stone. After that, he simply jumped off the top and landed on the grass. He'd let his senses guide him to the woman. She was moving fast, but not fast enough.

***

Morgan glanced over her shoulder and stopped in her tracks. "That can't be…I can't have gone so far." She was barely panting, but the perimeter lights triggered by the alarm were far back in the distance. At her best she could never run faster than a six-minute mile, and she'd only been running for a very short time. Rationalizing the speed by her desperate desire to get away, she didn't question the distance but turned to keep going. She only got another few hundred yards when an eerie feeling crept up her spine. She stopped again and listened. Sure her imagination was getting the best of her, she walked a few more feet and stared into a dark grove to her right. That was when she saw the eyes.

There were several sets glowing at her like small orbs at first. Then they got much bigger as their owners approached. Before she knew what was happening, something knocked her off her feet. She tried to get up, but several sets of hands held her down. A horrible face loomed over her. It was gaunt with fangs hanging from its upper jaw. Its ear tips were pointed, and the glowing eyes held a desperately maniacal look within their depths. The hands holding her down were more like claws and the rasping breathing of the creature nearest her was sickening and ominous. The thing's breath smelled like decaying flesh, an aroma common in her previous line of work.

"*Shit!*" she uttered and tried to free herself. Her absolute terror lent courage to her heart. She had to get away.

"A changeling," the voice hoarsely croaked. "Sean is losing his touch to let one so new leave his protection."

"Get off me!" she cried.

The thing stuck out its long tongue and licked the side of her neck and face. She growled in fury. "If you do that again, I'll hang your balls on my rearview mirror!"

"*Feisty*. And probably tasty," the thing told the others. "We must get her away from here before someone comes."

Morgan heard the same rasping sound of acknowledgment from the other creatures holding her down. She counted five—four on each of her limbs and the one hovering over her. If there was any doubt about vampires existing before, she quickly withdrew her previous suspicion.

"Let me go." She tried to pull free but it was like trying

to move hardening cement. She couldn't budge an inch.

"*Ohhhh*, do struggle, pretty one. It makes the prey so much more palatable," the leader of the pack snarled.

The thing opened its gaping jaw and Morgan knew she'd never see another day. Just as she braced herself for the inevitable bone-crushing bite that would take her head off, something hit the entity on top of her and sent it sprawling across the moor. The others quickly let her go and backed away. Morgan didn't dwell on what saved her but got up and started backing off. Her retreat was abruptly stopped by a very solid form standing to her rear.

Sean quickly shoved her behind him.

"Oh look…the kiddies have come out to play," he quipped.

Morgan gasped when the bony, despicable monsters in front of Sean pulled blades of varying sizes from beneath their black leather coats. They barely resembled men but she reasoned that's what they *had* been at one time.

The leader of the pack addressed Sean. "She's ours, *Nightwatcher*. You failed to keep her safe."

"Just one question before I send you to hell," Sean calmly spoke. "How did you know she was even here?"

"Maybe a little bird told us," the leader responded.

"Well, if that's the best answer you can give…bring it on, little man." Sean raised his hands and took a fighting stance.

Morgan moved to his left and grabbed his bicep. "Don't you think now would be a good time to *leave*?" she choked.

"Get behind me and stay there!" he ordered.

When the cadavers that were once men slowly approached with their blades lifted, Morgan backed up and did as Sean commanded. It was on the top of her mind to run. Every instinct told her to, but she couldn't leave her rescuer to fight by himself. Fairness dictated that she stay there and see this through—since she was the one who brought on the entire confrontation.

***

When one of the taller beings lunged, Sean kicked the blade from the monstrosity's hand, planted his fist in its face, and sent it reeling a good ten feet backward. Another one charged and he parried the blow by deflecting the arm holding the blade, circling around behind the attacker, and sending a hard punch into its left kidney. When the third one came at him, Sean was surprised by a sudden movement from behind. Morgan moved up and put a neat side-thrust kick into the creature's middle. As it stumbled backward, she followed up with a quick front snap kick to its groin. The two attackers left standing backed away. Predictably, the creatures didn't want to fight if it was fair. They liked to toy with their prey, believing the fear would make the meat tender.

"Another time, *Nightwatcher*."

Sean wasn't surprised by their use of the nickname. This particular pack of rogues had been around for centuries. They were familiar with the organization and his part in it. He watched as the two uninjured members of the pack picked up most of their compatriots and hauled them off, into the night. At the top of a small rise, they shape-shifted and the flock of bats they now became flew to the east. The one Morgan had unmanned with her kick to the groin was still on the ground, howling in pain. But he soon pushed himself into a standing position, loped into the woods and shapeshifted, fleeing before Sean could reach him.

Sean finally returned to her. Morgan was so intent on watching the bat-flying figures disappear, her full attention wasn't on him until he spoke.

"Do you always kick men in the *bahoogeys* like that?"

She finally faced him, gasped, and slowly backed up.

"What's the matter, Morgan? You'd think you'd never seen a vampire before." Sean joked, then put his hands on his hips, and waited for her to recover enough to speak.

She kept backing away until a tall, upright stone stopped her retreat. *"Oh…my…God!* Y-Your eyes are…are gglowing. And…you've got f-fangs."

"Ah…you *noticed.*"

She gazed toward the sky where her attackers had flown. "Wh-What were they? I thought they…they…"

"They're *rogues*. Feeding off vampires…living as cannibals for far too many years. That's what makes them look the way they do. Simply drinking our blood won't change us into what you just saw. Actually eating vampire flesh *does*. Their souls are putrid to the core. They care for nothing but themselves and hide in shadows. They can assume normal human form, which is how they can hide among mankind. But what you saw is their appearance in vampiric personae. Once they take on the stronger version of themselves, they can't hide the cannibal inside." Sean slowly stalked her down. "They love fresh meat. That's what a changeling is to them. And trust me when I tell you this…they don't leave any leftovers. Not even enough blood or tissue to test for DNA." After he finished his explanation, Morgan simply stood there and stared in wide-eyed silence.

"Don't you ever, *ever* leave the compound again unless I give you permission," he growled. "I don't know how they found you out here, in the middle of nowhere, but it's certain they can do it again. Had the alarm not sounded as soon as you got on the other side of the wall, your pretty little ass would be tonight's main course."

"There r-really are v-vampires," she brokenly whispered.

Sean tilted his head a moment before speaking. "Is that why you ran?" He briefly lowered his head and sighed heavily. "Christ almighty! You really *didn't* believe anything you were told on the damned plane…or anything Dani said to you."

She gripped the rock behind her. "I can't."

"I understand now. If you *do*, then I'm what you've become and you don't want to believe that either," he surmised.

She only shook her head and hung onto the rock for support.

"How do you think you ran so far in just a few minutes, Morgan? How do you think you got over the wall so easily? And how the bloody hell do you think you were able to knock down a creature with many times more strength than a human? It would take someone with special powers…the powers of a vampire."

"I…I'm not like them. If I am, then you should have let me die," she gasped.

Sean pinched the bridge of his nose between his thumb and forefinger and tried again. "I told you. They're *rogues*. They look like they do because they've been eating the flesh of other vampires. They're pure evil. They made the choice to be the way they are," he insisted. "They sometimes even eat humans if they can't find something they like better…like a changeling. They never had to live like this…they've *chosen* to."

When this didn't sink in, he tried again. "When you change, you'll look like I do right now. You'll have glowing eyes and elongated incisors…you won't be like…" he let his words trail away. She didn't seem capable of listening right now. She was shaking so badly that she couldn't move or speak. He was aware of her shock; it filtered through his senses like a jackhammer. For a moment, he felt compassion but quickly tamped it down.

"Come on. We need to get back to the compound before your little playmates get the nerve to try again. I'll have someone ferret that bunch out and destroy them before they ravage the countryside." When Sean took several steps away and Morgan didn't move, he turned back. "Morgan?" he prompted.

All she did was stare at him. Sean put his hands on either side of her face. The posture effectively trapped her against the standing stone. "I'm sorry. But this is the way it is. If you can't deal with it, you can always stay outside and let the sun come up on you. I've seen it happen and the cries of agony left me with the impression that it isn't a particularly pleasant way for a vampire to leave this life. But that's your other choice. It's the same choice you made when you and your partner broke through the door of that warehouse and you took the bullets from those drug runners. Now…what do you want to do?" The words had been softly but firmly spoken. Morgan stared at him a long moment more before responding.

"I'll go back with you," she quietly uttered.

"All right…let's go. But we're going to have a long talk. And I expect you to listen to every single word."

She simply nodded.

"Don't look at me like that, Morgan. You haven't been defeated, woman. Consider tonight a very hard lesson. Now, follow me," he tersely commanded.

***

"Oh, thank goodness she's all right." Dani ran forward

when they came through the front entrance. She put both her hands around Morgan's shoulders and hugged her.

"Take her to her room, Dani."

"Members from the head council called," Dani advised. "I told them you were out walking on the grounds with Morgan and you asked not to be disturbed. Fergus called, too, but said he'd ring again unless you contact him first."

Sean stiffened. "You said nothing else?"

The older woman shook her head. "I made it sound quite innocent. Very ordinary."

"Thanks, Dani."

"What's the council?" Morgan asked in a wooden tone.

Sean moved closer to her and lifted her downcast chin with one finger. "It's a group of supervisory staff heading up the agency. Fergus MacArtan is the leader. He's an *ancient*. I told you about their kind on the plane, though I don't know you'd remember in the state you were in. In fact, Fergus and his people started *Nightwatchers* many years ago. That call was to see how you're getting along, how you're adjusting so far. It's procedure he'd check in with me after bringing an initiate home."

"What will you say? Didn't you tell me my uncle would be in serious trouble if they found out I didn't want this?"

It wasn't the question she asked so much as the look in her eyes that got to him. She was afraid for Patrick—not for herself but for her uncle. "I'll think of something. Just go upstairs with Dani and get cleaned up." He swiped at a dark smudge of mud on her left cheek.

When Morgan moved away, she only took a couple of steps up the stairway then stopped and looked back down at Sean. "Don't let them hurt my uncle…*please*!"

Sean didn't answer. Dani prodded Morgan into moving up the stairs, but he didn't miss the alarmed look on *Dani's* face. It was equal to the dread on Morgan's. He quickly walked into his study, closed the doors, and made the phone call. A strong, powerful voice echoed into the private line.

"MacArtan here."

"Fergus, it's Sean Reilly. I understand you called while I was out, sir."

"Good to hear from you, Sean. As per procedure, Patrick made his initial contact with me and said things are moving along splendidly in California. How's the woman?"

Sean prayed he could pull this off. "She's one of a kind, sir, top form."

"*Excellent*. If you would, make her training a priority. I'll be assigning some of your cases elsewhere until she's able to handle field ops."

That bit of news made Sean clench his free hand in frustration.

"I'd also like to stop by Greenwood to meet her when I can get some damned files off my desk, and work slows a bit," Fergus continued.

"Just let us know when you'll be coming, sir. We'll

have your usual room ready and Morgan's progress report up-to-the-minute."

"I'll get back to you. Just keep Morgan under your wing." Fergus paused and changed subjects. "It must be good to be back in Ireland."

"Of *course*. I miss it even when I'm gone for a brief time," Sean congenially replied.

"Very well. Keep up the excellent work. I'll have my people get you a schedule as soon as my plans are confirmed."

"Goodnight, Mr. MacArtan."

"And to you, Sean."

Sean put the receiver down and leaned against the desk. If word of what happened tonight got back to MacArtan Castle, Morgan might just as well be in her coffin and Patrick with her. He looked up at the ceiling, in the direction of Morgan's room, and decided the talk he was going to put off until tomorrow night couldn't wait. He purposefully strode from the study and up the stairs.

***

Morgan sat on the edge of her bed after finishing her shower. The cream and pale green room was the loveliest place she'd ever seen. An antique armoire sat in the corner, pastoral oil paintings hung on the walls, a television as well as a refrigerator for the ever-necessary blood Dani kept pestering her to drink were also part of the decor. There was even a private bathroom complete with a clawfoot tub. As splendid as the room was, she found it impossible to focus on her surroundings for more than a few moments. Her brain was crowded with all the input from the last few days. From having been shot to dealing with becoming a vampire, everything was like a B-rated movie with *her* as the poorly cast star. As she sat quietly, Danielle towel dried her hair. The older woman had been kind but unusually quiet. "Aren't you going to give me the third degree about leaving the compound?" Morgan finally asked.

Dani shook her head. "No, Morgan, I'm not. This has

been a dreadful week for you, and it's time to just forget it and put it behind us."

"Sean didn't tell you we ran into what he called rogues." She heard Dani gasp and continued. "Dani…I saw Sean the way he really is. His eyes were glowing…it was like they were on fire or something." She paused for a moment. "Will I look like that, too?"

Dani shook her head and made a *tsking* sound. "Oh, my dear girl…you should *never* have left the compound. Rogues love to prey on newly changed vampires. I don't know why they were so close, but you have to be very, very careful, Morgan. Even the strongest vampires never go out without a weapon of some kind, and they keep their wits about them," Dani warned. "I assume Sean took care of them."

"He scared them off, if that's what you mean." She noted Dani hadn't answered her question about *her* own physical transformation into vampirism. "If Sean hadn't been there, I'd have been an entree."

“That’s not entirely true,” Sean spoke from the open doorway. “You managed to kick one of those rotting bastards until he couldn’t stand straight. His stones will hurt all night.”

Dani smiled at Morgan and said, “See…you *can* fight back.”

Morgan instinctively pulled her robe tighter. Sean took a deep breath and let it out slowly.

“Excuse us for a few minutes, Dani. I need to speak with Morgan alone.”

Dani got up to leave but paused as she passed Sean. She opened her mouth to say something but, at a stern look from her boss, she quickly snapped it shut.

***

When the older woman left the room, Sean closed the bedroom door and slowly walked toward Morgan. “That was a hell of a stunt you pulled. Are you always so brash?”

“They used to call me *Morgan the Mauler* back at the department.”

He tried not to smile, but the nickname suited her. "Odd, that moniker wasn't mentioned in your file but I'll keep it in mind." Sean slowly picked up a chair, turned it around, and straddled it. "How are you feeling?"

"What do you want me to say?"

"It's a simple question."

She shrugged. "I don't know…I don't know how I feel."

Sean paused, then decided to tell her. "I just got off the phone with Fergus MacArtan. He wants to meet you."

She stared at him. "He'll know I don't want to be here, won't he?"

"He will unless you get your act together, Morgan. I can't help you if you won't help yourself. And that means Patrick will go down with you…do you understand?"

"I was a cop," she whispered, "not a vampire. I don't know how to do this."

"I can teach you…if you're willing to learn. Patrick

seemed to think you'd accept this."

"My uncle would have told you anything to keep me alive…*if* you can call this living."

"Promise me there won't be a repeat of what you did tonight," he demanded.

"I think you can tattoo it on my forehead!"

"I've got to go out tonight. Can I trust you?"

Morgan slowly nodded. "I just told you, I won't be leaving here again…not without permission and not without a weapon."

"Good. I'll have Dani show you the armory tomorrow night. We can see what you'd like in the way of protection."

"Is it really safe for you to be leaving after what happened? Won't those things want to eat you?" she softly asked.

"The rogues and I have had our little setbacks from time to time. But they don't mess with me unless I'm protecting their prey…or getting in their way."

She looked down at her clasped hands. "I get your point. I was the prey."

Sean silently considered her for a long moment. "I heard what you asked Dani…about my appearance." There was absolute silence. "Does it repel you so much?"

"I…It's not like I've got anything to compare it to," she quietly reasoned.

With her head down, all that brown hair spilling over her shoulders, and the gentle curve of her breasts visible where the robe had slipped open, her appearance made him aware of how long it'd been since he'd had a woman. But he quickly brought his mind back to the subject.

"If you think I'm bad, Morgan, there are some truly evil things in this world. Things you'd find *much* less palatable. The rogues are just a taste of evil. There's much worse out there, believe me. Even a former police officer wouldn't know what I mean."

She looked up then. "*How*? How could anything be

worse than that?"

Memories flooded through him. "I remember seeing humans preying on other humans. It was the most sickening thing you can imagine."

"I don't *think* so. There couldn't be any group of humans so—"

"It was a place called Buchenwald," Sean softly interrupted. "And you can't *remotely* know how truly evil a thing is until you've seen a place like that." With this comment hanging, he got up and left her to think.

***

Sean drove his motorcycle up to the alley entrance of the pub.

Thor's Hammer was the one place in the world where he could get help without letting the council know what was happening. It was common for him to drink there. Tonight would seem no different to any agents who might be happening by.

Inside, he'd find the one man he could tell the truth.

He quickly parked the bike, pulled off his helmet and went through the back entrance. A vampire guard at the rear of the pub nodded in acknowledgment. The guards knew who he was and wouldn't try to stop him from seeing Skord Shorner, formerly Skord *Proust*. The two of them had maintained their strong friendship. Even after the war ended so many decades ago.

As Sean entered the main part of the bar, a very large man stood from where he'd been seated and motioned for *him* to take a chair. Sean did so and waited for their server to supply him and his host with two pewter flagons of fresh red blood.

"What brings you here, my friend?" Skord asked as he picked up his own flagon.

"I need a favor. You're the only one I can trust."

"Sounds serious."

"It is. I…I can't let the agency know about this, Skord.

It's between you and me."

"You know my relationship with the *agency*. They won't find out anything from my end. But what could be so wrong that you'd breach security and talk business to a former operative?"

Sean looked around. There was a mixture of vampires and humans in the bar. The humans, of course, didn't know who their fellow carousers were or that other reddish drinks being served *weren't* wine.

After the war, his old friend had done exactly as he wanted and set himself up with a series of bars, pubs, and restaurants across Europe. Sean assumed Skord did quite well if the current patronage was any indication. He surveyed the room closely and waited for a vampiric waitress to finish refilling his glass before continuing. "Do you remember Patrick Grady?"

"Of course," Skord admitted. "Good man. I thought he was out of the organization."

"He was," Sean confirmed, "but he called in an initiation, as procedure allows. The problem is, Pat never told his recruit about the agency or that vampires even exist."

Skord had his pewter flagon halfway to his lips but froze. "I remember what the rules used to say about that."

"They're the same. That's why the council can't find out." Sean paused and leaned forward. "To make matters worse, the bloody idiot's recruit was his own niece."

Skord held up one hand to stop Sean from saying more and motioned for their waitress to leave a full pewter pitcher of blood on their table before speaking. "What's the rest of the story, Sean? What *aren't* you telling me?"

Sean took Morgan's old file photo out of his leather coat pocket and slid it across the table to Skord. "I got this from her personnel records."

Skord looked it over. "She's in uniform…a policewoman? American?"

"Yeah," Sean confirmed. "She was working undercover

with the LAPD. I made some calls and found out an investigation is underway; her supervisors think an informant sold her out." He sipped some of his blood before continuing. "To get to the point…she was shot and was dying. Patrick panicked and called me in to save her. I brought her back to Greenwood," he paused, shook his head and added, "She hasn't taken her change well. We'd just got back from the airport when the little *banshee* escaped over the compound wall and ran. I brought her back, but not before a pack of rogues found her out on the hills. I had to *persuade* them to move along."

Skord snorted and half-smiled. "No one can say you lead a dull life, my friend." He looked at the photo again. "Beautiful woman…very nice indeed."

Sean took the picture when his friend handed it back. "I need to know why those rogues were close to the safe house. Morgan was only a few miles away when they found her."

Skord knocked the ashes from his cigar. "It sounds like

something Regar would cook up."

"I thought of that. Since when did he align himself with rogues?"

"You never know what he'd do, Sean. He was only predictable in his fixated hostility toward the organization. That was all any of us ever knew about him." Skord took a sip of his blood. "I'll put out alerts; let the others know there are rogues lurking. I'm sure if anyone sees them, I'll hear about it. But there's just one thing."

"Yes?"

"Since I'm out of the organization, you know that I occasionally check in like the good little agent I *was*," he acerbically stated. "But the phone I use for *baby-sitting* purposes certainly isn't secure. I know that Danielle is still with you and she can be trusted. I assume, since it's Patrick's niece we're talking about, that Dani knows what happened," Skord reasoned. "The point I'm getting at is unless things have changed the landlines in and out of Greenwood aren't private. Even if Dani or you use some kind of coded language, someone listening in will know that something is up. I can't have access to private cell numbers. The organization used to take a dim view of their even being used, so we can't take that chance. Finally, I've certainly got no business showing up at any safe house."

"Yes, I *know*. No one minds us being friends as long we meet in public places and there's no exchange of agency information," Sean expounded wearily and ran one hand across his face in aggravation.

"It's the rules, Sean. We both know it. The problem is…if you want the help, I'll need some way to contact you quickly…a way Fergus and his people can't monitor."

"As you've said, there isn't any means of communication that can be considered secure."

Skord grinned, then surreptitiously glanced sideways and said, "Neither are we."

"What do you mean?"

"Two agents just walked into the pub. They're at the far end of the bar, ordering from Molly."

Sean carefully glanced where his friend indicated and saw two large men being waited on by a buxom blonde. The men were wearing dark glasses, even though the sun was down, and both sported black suits with white shirts and black ties. Their garments stood out in a sea of jean-clad relaxed patrons. The agents, if one could refer to them thus, were veritable poster boys for Spies-R- Us.

"*Sweet Jesus and St. Joseph!* Where the shaggin' hell is Fergus recruiting from these days…Hollywood? Those two may as well hang signs on their damned backs. I can almost smell 'em they're so green."

"Fergus has been keeping watch on me," Skord announced.

Sean stared at his comrade. "Why would he…why the shaggin' hell wasn't I told?" Anger edged his questions.

"Fergus knows we stay in touch. He wouldn't want to

offend *you* by revealing he was having your best friend watched."

"But why? Neither of us is breakin' any rules! At least…not until tonight," Sean sheepishly admitted.

"It doesn't matter," Skord replied straightforwardly. "We could lose *those* rookies in our sleep," he assured his friend while shaking his head in denial. "This isn't what you think, Sean. Fergus doesn't believe for a minute that you'd pass on information outside the agency or that I'd abuse it. His interest is in getting me back," Skord asserted. "Though it's beneath his dignity to beg or to have you do so on his behalf, sending those agents here is a way to remind me…persistently…that the organization is out there and I can rejoin at any time. It's Fergus's way of staying in my face. He's done it before."

Sean stared at his big best friend. "Why haven't you said something?"

Skord smiled impishly. "It'd have only pissed you

off…the way it just did. Besides, I like walking out of here and letting his underlings follow me. I lead them all over Dublin, then ditch them in some bizarre place like a whorehouse or a waste treatment plant. It drives them crazy and keeps me amused."

Sean's shoulders shook with mirth. "Why does that sound *exactly* like something you'd do?"

"Look, I can make this easy on everyone," Skord said as he stroked his chin in thought. "Just let it be known that I'm considering re-joining. Have Dani send an unassuming, but widely broadcast memo to this effect. If she happens to receive a logged memorandum from *you* telling *her* to contact me with a list of agency numbers, Fergus and the rest of the supervisors will assume you're trying to bring me back in."

"That could actually work."

"I believe it will. No one will even *ask* about the breach of procedure," Skord declared. "I say this with all humility, Sean…Fergus would do anything to get me back. More to the point, if I have access to all the landlines, I can relay any information about those rogues in such a way that no one, including supervisors, will know what the hell I'm talking about. I'll use metaphors the way I used to during the war and we had to communicate on unsecured phones. No one will link conversations to your changeling's contact with rogues, or with Patrick's indiscretion. Fergus will let abnormal commentary slide. As long as it's all associated with getting me back," he reiterated.

Sean couldn't find a single flaw in his friend's resourcefulness. For a second, he flashed back to World War II. It was like they were in some hotel room plotting another covert op. He was amazed at how easily it all came back. Moreover, it reminded him that Skord Shorner was a master at this game. He knew no one understood the covert world better. The entire conversation led him to ask a pertinent question. "*Are* you considering coming back?"

His large friend remained silent for so long that Sean

almost repeated the query.

"Seems to me that if things don't work out with Patrick's niece and she can't accept what's she's become…you'll need to send her someplace safe, Sean. The only other option you have is to kill her."

Sean glanced down at Morgan's picture. He knew the rules as well as Skord.

"If Fergus actually believed I wanted to come back into the agency, I could always say I thought it over long and hard, then changed my mind for some reason. You could report your changeling wouldn't make it as an agent though she tried. You might even suggest that she just couldn't hack the training, or the psychological changes brought on by vampirism. She could agree to sever all contact, meeting all the agency's requirements for doing so. And then the two of us could take off. Fergus *might* buy the entire ruse. But even if he didn't, you wouldn't suffer for it. I'll claim you knew nothing about the woman wanting to come with me, that she and I struck up a romantic relationship and decided to leave everything behind. And with my network, I can keep her safe from the council members and the rogues; at least until she's ready to go out on her own. In this way, no one would find out about Patrick's deception. As I see it, this might be the only choice you have besides taking the girl outside the compound and letting the sun come up on her."

Sean knew his friend was absolutely right but couldn't reconcile the trouble Skord would willingly accept. "Why would you put yourself through all that? I was told when you left, members of the organization allowed you extraordinary latitude. You were one of their very best agents and your behavior proved you could be trusted. Why would you risk destroying that trust, possibly getting on the bad side of Fergus MacArtan…all for some woman you don't even know?"

Skord sipped more blood before answering. "I've been around for a very long time, my friend, and I've enjoyed the company of thousands of women. But it's once in a lifetime you come across a woman like *this,*" he answered slowly. "Just by seeing her image, I can tell she's different. There's something in her eyes which is very rare. And it's said the eyes are the keys to the soul." Skord shrugged noncommittally. "Let's just say…if she looks half as good now as she did in that old picture, she might be very grateful. Grateful enough that we could make a very good…*team.*"

Something in the vicinity of Sean's heart tightened. Skord loved beautiful women and always had his pick of them. Morgan being among that lot wasn't to his taste for some reason. "And what are you going to do if she decides to stay with the organization?"

He shrugged. "For a woman who looks like that, I might really consider coming back. Given Fergus's attempts to hold my interest, I might have her assigned to my safe house as an enlistment condition," he mused. "Indeed, she might like Austria this time of year. As you know, there's a very comfortable safe house there…isolated in the mountains. It's quite romantic for an agency holding."

Sean watched him closely. He'd never seen his friend look so wistful when speaking about a female, and he believed him to be dead serious. In fact, he'd never seen the gentle giant quite so latched on a plan. In truth, the only thing he'd ever seen Skord more concerned with was killing Nazis. His friend's surname might have changed over the years, but his intensity over that particular subject hadn't.

Sean drank the rest of his blood. "I'll be leaving now. Let me know if you find out anything about those rogues. I'll have Dani contact you with the access numbers."

Skord stood when Sean did. "You never told me what the woman's name was."

"Morgan Grady," Sean reluctantly supplied.

Skord smirked. "I'll expect an introduction."

Sean nodded, quickly thanked him for the fresh blood, and stalked back to his motorcycle.

Skord was the best friend he'd ever had. But how the man could get so intrigued by an old photo was ridiculous. With a league of vampire beauties at his beck and call, what was the big German's sudden and intense interest in Morgan? Standing by the bike, Sean pulled the photo out and looked at it again. He considered her bright smile, the way her eyes lit up, and the tilt of her head when the picture had been taken. She *was* beautiful and even more so in person. Strikingly so.

He shoved the picture back into his pocket, pulled on his helmet and headed back to Greenwood. Why did he give a damn what Skord did or didn't want? His suggested plan might have been a way to get Patrick and Morgan off the hook, but it was foolish to assume the council and Fergus MacArtan would fall for it. And if they didn't and they began asking questions concerning Morgan's change, all this would have been for nothing. Morgan might be subjected to the council's whim.

What Skord didn't know was one of the rules *had* been

changed.

Any agent considered unsafe to the organization was to be located, taken into custody immediately, and executed before witnesses. The logic was simple; it was to make sure the deed was done humanely and to guarantee there was no trace of the offending agent's existence. Traitors, should they ever rear their head, would think twice about revealing *Nightwatchers* as an organization or compromising the identities of those in its service. The ease of communicating around the world in seconds had made this rule necessary.

Those agents now retired or living in the outside world with permission, like Skord, had no need to know about this regulation as long as they weren't a threat. Everyone in the agency, and still responsible for duties each day, knew about the directive and agreed to it. Its existence kept them and their families protected.

As he rode, Sean realized Skord might be subjected to this edict if his plan failed. In fact, every friend he had might end up facing execution…right beside him.

For the life of him, he didn't know why he hadn't told Skord about the *Termination Alert*, as the regulation was titled. Maybe he secretly hoped the alternate plan would work and his pub-owning friend could spirit Morgan away. Still, nothing they did would matter if Morgan wouldn't agree to *act* as if she'd been recruited the right way. If he could actually convince her to stay with the organization, that would be the best solution.

He felt the need to get back to Greenwood as soon as possible. His urgency wasn't prompted because the sun would be up soon, but because he felt he hadn't thoroughly warned Morgan about the light.

He regretted suggesting sunlight was one way of ending her vampirism; if eternal life was too difficult to except. Acting on the idea, she might be able to fight off the morning lethargy she'd experience. Having accomplished this, she might try to leave her room and go outside or at least open a shade somewhere in the house. And while it would solve all *his* problems, the thought of her doing something so horrendous was chilling. He pushed the custom-made motorcycle to its limit, to get back. Greenwood was still miles away.

Chapter 4

Sean bolted up the stairs and to the hallway where his and Morgan's rooms were safely closed from the sun. In less than fifteen minutes, night would fall away and dawn would appear. As he hurried down the long hall, he felt a supreme surge of relief. Danielle was seated on a sofa outside Morgan's room with some of her endless paperwork in her lap. She looked up and smiled when she detected his presence. Sean thanked heaven Dani was as perceptive and loyal as anyone he'd ever supervised. "I take it she's in her room and didn't try anything else?"

Dani nodded, put her paperwork aside and stood. "She told me she'd stay put and said she promised you the same thing. But seeing as this is her first night in the compound, I thought I'd stay near."

Sean glanced at her door. "What about the guards? They knew she tried to escape."

"It's taken care of, Sean. I simply told them that Morgan was so captivated by her new powers that she took a climb over the wall and went for a run. And I reminded them you go walking outside the compound occasionally."

"What was their response?"

Dani waved a careless hand. "They laughed it off and reset the alarm. I told them you went out to join her…to teach her some of her new powers."

Sean frowned. "They shouldn't have been so easily fooled."

"They trust me to tell them the truth or they wouldn't have been. But I had to say something that would keep word of this from getting back to MacArtan Castle and the council."

"After those rogues almost took Morgan out, I don't think we'll need to worry about her going over the wall again."

Dani eyed him curiously. "Then why were you in such a rush just now? It looked as if you couldn't wait to get here."

He shrugged and turned his face away. "She makes me nervous. I'm not sure she won't pull some other stunt."

"Hmmm."

Sean quickly turned his head back toward Danielle. "What're you thinking, Dani?"

"Nothing," She picked up her paperwork again. "I'll let you get to your room. You only have a few minutes left. Sleep well."

Sean stood there as Danielle walked away. She usually kept the same hours as he; sleeping the better part of the day and arising in the afternoon before him to get an early start on paperwork. There was no reason to believe Dani would come near Morgan's door again.

He waited until she was out of sight, then raised his hand to knock on Morgan's door. After finding out vampires existed, that she was one of them and doing her best to escape, the newest member of the household had been eerily subdued. Before his fist could contact the wood, the door swung open and the subject of his thoughts stood in the doorframe.

"I thought I heard you," she softly commented. "Where did Dani go?"

"To bed. It's been a long night, and she probably didn't get much sleep on the trip."

He noticed that Morgan now wore a silk robe wrapped tightly around her slender body. Her long hair swung around her shoulders. The haphazard way it hung made him want to plunge his hands into the shimmering mass. His keen sense of smell indicated that she was wearing something citrus-based or had washed her hair with some kind of botanical shampoo. He could smell lemon. It was one of his favorite scents.

"I…I didn't thank you, Sean. If you hadn't shown up, I'd be dead. Or whatever it is that happens to vampires when rogues get their hands on one."

"They won't always be looking for you. It's just that they can sense a changeling and find them if they're nearby.

Changelings have a different odor."

Morgan shook her head. "Like what?"

He exhaled slowly and shrugged. "It's…it's like smelling a new baby. I can't explain it any other way."

"Oh," Morgan uttered. "I was just wondering why they happened to be out there when I went over the wall. I mean, there's nobody for them to…*eat*…out there at night. Is there? It just seemed strange to me."

"I'm not exactly sure why they were in the vicinity. I've got a friend checking on it. But until you're trained and ready, I don't want another repeat of tonight's escapade. Dani lied to the guards so they thought you were innocently fooling around."

"I didn't think I'd be back here. What the guards thought didn't matter when I went over the wall."

"What the guards and everyone else believes is vitally important, Morgan." He moved closer. "They have to believe you're here because you want to be. If my superiors find out what Patrick did—"

She held up one hand. "I know. They won't find out. I'll behave from now on. I've already told you I would."

"But you don't like any part of this."

She shook her head. "I didn't have a choice. Because of it, I'm not sure I want to see my uncle."

That surprised him. "No matter how you dislike the situation, Patrick saved you from the grave. That's where you'd be right now."

"I know. But I don't know if I can be a member of your agency. For all I know, *The Nightwatchers* might be comprised of a lot of sinister people with ulterior motives. Just the idea that a vampire could be good is an oxymoron, isn't it?"

"Do you think Dani is evil? Or your uncle?"

"Uncle Pat has lied to me about his whole life. So far, Dani seems as loyal to you as any soldier. But my uncle's dishonesty and your assistant's devotion doesn't improve my situation or my opinion. If anything…their behavior makes me think you people will do whatever it takes to get your way. So if my attitude isn't all that accommodating, consider their actions and add to it the dire warnings I've been given. Am I supposed to think you're operating in my best interests…right after you tell me I could be murdered?" Morgan sternly asked.

"The members of the council are good people, Morgan. But they have to keep all the rest of their employees safe. We have staff in some very vulnerable positions all over the world. One wrong word to the wrong source could put those men and women in mortal danger. And without those agents being where they are, the world could be close to catastrophe. We're currently watching different arms buyers, the illegal market, and anyone trying to get their hands on biological or nuclear weapons or the components to make them. We operate much the same way you would when undercover. It's just that the stakes are much higher. And sometimes our operatives have got to do what they've got to do. This work is rarely pleasant, but we look to the greater good and see how many innocent people we can keep safe. The countries under our protection depend on us."

"And what made you want to do this? What's in it for you?"

"The safety of the free world—"

"No," she interrupted, "I want to know what *you* get out of this, Sean. I was a cop because I wanted to help people. But I found out early on that I got an incredible rush from my job. It made me feel alive and special. That kind of power is addicting. So why do *you* do this?"

For a moment, he was surprised into speechlessness. He simply stood there staring at her. A very old pain flared in the vicinity of his heart. "Have a good rest, Morgan. The sun is almost up, and I need to get to my room. When you awaken, stay where you are. I'll get you."

She simply shrugged and slowly closed the door.

***

As soon as the last rays of sun left the landscape, Sean was pulled into consciousness. Instead of calling Danielle to his room as usual and lounging in his bathrobe until the daily paperwork was tackled, he quickly rose, showered and dressed. He then made his way to Morgan's room. When he saw her door cracked open and heard Dani's familiar voice mingling with Morgan's, he slowed his pace and lingered in the hallway. Eavesdropping wasn't his style, but he did it anyway, convincing himself that it was only to hear if Morgan was in a better mood.

"I can't believe you drove all the way to Dublin and bought this stuff! Didn't you get any sleep?" Morgan asked.

"I got up early and couldn't resist the temptation. You've such a lovely figure, and no offense meant, but I was the one who packed your clothing at your apartment. It was a little lacking. So, I checked your tags for sizes…intending to get you some appropriate clothes."

"You mean I dressed like an underpaid, overworked

cop. Like all my friends."

Sean heard a moment of silence, and he could imagine Morgan was remembering her friends and missing them. Obviously, Dani had done some shopping. The task might have been necessary if Morgan were a permanent resident, but it wasn't likely she'd be around much longer. Dani's kindheartedness was beyond the call of duty. He heard rustling. It was shortly followed by Morgan's awed voice.

"This dress is awesome, Dani."

"The color is perfect. I knew it would be, but then it'd look smashing on your figure, even if the fabric was burlap. You're every bit as lovely as Patrick told me. He's so proud of you," Dani proclaimed.

Silence again. Sean waited for the conversation to continue, but he didn't feel guilty about eavesdropping. Morgan couldn't yet sense his presence in the hallway because she was new to vampirism and she hadn't yet learned to tap into her deeper supernatural instincts.

"I love my uncle very much. I just wish he'd told me about all this," Morgan quietly asserted.

"Well, that makes two of us."

"Do you mean that you wished he'd told me about all this to include the agency and that vampires exist…or that you're in love him?" Morgan pointedly asked.

"Both," Dani admitted. "What gave me away?"

"You've been talking about Uncle Pat non-stop since you came in my room. The expression on your face is the same I have when I eat chocolate," Morgan gently teased.

"I *do* love your uncle. We've been in love for a number of years. We worked out of this safe house and other places with Sean."

"If you don't mind me asking, why didn't you and Uncle Pat ever marry? Isn't that permitted?"

"Oh yes. We've quite a number of agents, both human and vampire, who are married or live together."

"Then why—" Morgan's words stopped but then

started back. "Uncle Pat came home to take care of me when my parents died. I was just a kid. You two would be together otherwise, wouldn't you?" After a moment of silence, Morgan continued. "I know this is very personal, but I have to get some things cleared up."

"I'll answer any question I can, dear."

"Would…would you and my uncle have become vampires and have carried on with your lives together… if not for his coming to the States to raise me?"

In the hallway, Sean stood absolutely still. He knew the answer to the question but hadn't ever heard Dani speak of these issues.

Dani took a deep breath before answering. "Yes. We planned to be together forever. Obviously, it would have been impossible for a vampire to take care of a little girl who was still in school, attending parties and sports events."

"And…he stayed in the States all these years to be near me. Because I *asked* him to," Morgan surmised and then followed with, "I didn't know anything about you and him…I'm sorry, Dani. You've been parted for years because of *me.*"

Sean could imagine the scene. Morgan and Danielle were probably hugging. He could almost sense the warmth of the embrace from where he stood. It had been a long time since any act of such empathy and tenderness had been played out under this old roof.

"It's all right, Morgan. You couldn't have known. You were just a child. Patrick had to go to you. There was nothing else that could be done," Dani offered.

"Yes, but I selfishly kept him to myself even after I was old enough to be on my own. I never thought about what *he* might want; that there might be somebody in his life that he couldn't tell me about."

"Patrick loves you dearly, my girl. More than you can ever imagine. He'd have done anything for you."

"What will you both do now?" Morgan softly asked.

"When Patrick gets here from the States, we want to take up our lives where we left off. I was rarely able to see him when he was gone. I spoke to him on the phone every month and on the internet of course. We were allowed that contact. But it's different from being together. We missed each other terribly."

"You stayed in love…even after all these years—"

"Love like that doesn't diminish, dear. It only grows with time. Haven't you ever been so in love with a man that you'd do anything for him?"

"I never met anybody that *did it* for me. Guess it just wasn't in the cards," Morgan slowly replied.

Sean eased closer and cautiously glanced in the room. Through the crack in the door he saw that Dani's hands were on either side of the younger woman's face. Dani was smiling at Morgan. He heard his assistant speak much softer but with her heart in her words.

"Morgan…for you not to have had someone special in

your life means there have to be some very stupid men out there."

Morgan hugged her. "I'm so glad you're here, Dani. I don't know what I'd do without you." Then she quickly got up to hunt for a tissue.

Sean heard that last whispered comment as he moved back from the door. He sensed the trust forming between the two women. And he envied them.

Women had the ability to bond so much more easily than most men. His relationships were alliances of power. Skord was his best friend because they first knew each other while fighting against terrible odds. Only later had the more natural male bonds asserted themselves. But Dani and Morgan had connected very quickly. Maybe it was their mutual love for Patrick. Despite Morgan's claim that she didn't want to see her uncle, she still loved him. The entire conversation between the two women made Sean suddenly long for something he couldn't name; something he hadn't had in a long time. Before he could dwell on it, he walked closer to the half-opened door, knocked, and pushed it wider without waiting for a response.

"Sean. It's good to see you up. I was just coming in with today's memos," Dani said as she swiped at a stray tear.

Sean tried not to notice that she'd been crying. It had been a very long time since he'd seen Dani in tears. He turned his attention to the other side of the room where Morgan now stood. In that moment, he felt as if the floor had just opened up. He tried not to let his jaw drop in obvious lust, but he wasn't sure the effort paid off.

Morgan had been transformed into the quintessential vampire warrior. She wore a tight, vee-neck black sweater, equally tight, black leather pants, and tall black riding boots. It was the clothing of their kind. The garments distinguished them as authoritative, and enemies would do well to steer clear. Humans would stay out of their way because, dressed as Morgan was now, they looked like they had sinister, even deadly connections.

Her eyes had been accented by smoky shadow, and the rest of her makeup only accentuated her flawless beauty. He surmised the application had been supervised by Dani, indicating a further close bonding between the women.

Try as he would, he couldn't dispel his body's response to all that femininity, grace and elegance. The leather only made her seem more *there*. He tried to cover his amazement with a topic of business. "If you're up to it, I'll take you to the armory and familiarize you with some weapons you might not have utilized before."

Morgan nodded. "After meeting up with those rogues, I'd *better* learn a lot more."

Satisfied with her answer, he tore his gaze away from Morgan's slender body and back to Dani. "Make sure Skord Shorner has access to our numbers from now on. I need you to email yourself a memo from my computer saying I gave you orders to authorize phone contact." He couldn't miss the expression of pleasure on Dani's face.

"Oh, Sean! Is Skord coming back?"

"Let's just say the council probably won't have a problem with him calling Greenwood. But notify MacArtan Castle. If Fergus has any questions about it I'll speak to him personally. I want there to be a clear connection, concerning Skord's phone access, linked back to my computer. Got it?"

Dani clasped her hands in glee. "I'm sure Mr. MacArtan will be ecstatic, Sean. Oh, it would be a wonderful career boost if you could get him to rejoin."

"I'm not so sure I can. But he'll be a reliable ally if things here don't work out," he said and pointedly looked back at Morgan. "He's also checking his sources for information concerning local rogues."

"I'll make sure Skord has those access numbers as soon as possible." Dani picked up her electronic notepad, jotted down a few reminders, and smiled at them as she left the room.

Sean looked back at Morgan. If it was possible, she seemed even more striking than before. Her hair had been pulled straight back and hung across one shoulder in a long ponytail. Professional but very feminine. "I'll meet you at the south end of the hallway in about fifteen minutes. Don't bother changing clothes. What you have on is more-or-less the working uniform."

Morgan glanced down at her clothing. "You guys like leather?"

He shrugged. "It suits us…no pun intended."

"I was wondering why Danielle insisted I wear this."

"Fifteen minutes," Sean reminded, then strode away.

***

Morgan glanced toward the small refrigerator in her room. Dani had made her drink an entire bottle of blood earlier. And the more she had, the less barbaric she found the notion of consuming it. "What the hell," she grumbled, then walked to the fridge, and took out another bottle. She was just finishing it when the requisite fifteen minutes had passed.

Closing her door behind her, she walked out of her room and down the hallway. Where Sean had told her to wait was by an elevator. She assumed that's where they'd have to go to get to the armory. It wouldn't make sense to have one on an upper floor if a basement were available. Not a moment later, Sean exited his room wearing black leather garments very similar to hers. His long hair was now loose, and the zipper on his black jacket had been left open. Underneath, he wore some kind of low-cut T-shirt showing a great deal of his chest. The muscles alone would have made her stare, but it was the dark tan of his skin that had her inappropriately blurting her next comment.

"I thought vampires were all pale and emaciated."

He raised one brow, punched the button to the elevator, and followed her inside it before answering. "I think I've got some Mediterranean blood in me. It's one of a few stereotypes that don't fit. The notion of looking like a

Hollywood monster is highly inaccurate."

"*Highly*," Morgan softly agreed, as she looked him over again.

"We don't float down a stairway and into the foyer wearing a cape and tuxedo. When we shapeshift, we don't magically appear that way, either."

"So, what *does* happen?"

"Our clothes fall off during shapeshifting. Hollywood notwithstanding, our powers don't extend to altering clothing. Wherever you find yourself after a shift, you'll be nude when reappearing in human form. That's why I *strongly* suggest you pay attention when being taught that particular power."

Using a bad accent in an attempt to speak like a movie vampire, Morgan asked, "Do we not don hoods or cryptic black coffin wear?"

He tried to suppress a smile. "The leather is about as cryptic as it gets."

"And who decided on the leather?" she queried in her

normal voice again.

"It's sort of our trademark. We can't exactly walk around in those tuxedos now, can we? At least not without being noticed."

And do you think you're not noticed?

She stared at him and wondered why somebody didn't just give her some blue jeans and an old flannel shirt she wore when she went undercover. While this gear was certainly evocative of a dangerous individual, whose presence wasn't to be taken lightly, it was also just as eye-catching as the trademark tuxedo. Still, she did like the way the leather felt when it conformed to her body. She wished she could at least see herself in a mirror so Dani's assertion that she was '*smashing*' could be confirmed. But something in Sean's gaze told her those words were true.

Morgan was used to men looking at her. But Sean's surreptitious perusal was as hot as any stare she'd ever received. Something in her responded positively and she wasn't sure this was a good thing. She tried to convince herself that her rise in anticipation was due to learning she actually *could* shift into different forms and possibly fly into the night. If the rogues could do it, she could.

But that wasn't the real reason for her sudden interest in what Sean was saying. It was more like the man himself held her riveted attention, whether she wanted to give it or not.

When the elevator door opened, Sean motioned for her to go first. She knew he was watching her as she exited and looked over the indoor firing range. It was built perpendicular to a long hallway. What she saw, even in a cursory glance, was the most modern shooting range she'd ever come across. Everything was spick and span. The hallway itself was battleship gray. The floor was polished white marble. She was pretty damn sure that she could eat off it if she'd still been human and sanitary conditions were an issue.

The range itself was painted all black; the lane targets

were clearly illuminated. "Some set up," Morgan announced. "You people don't skimp on anything, do you?"

"If you want the best agents, you pay them well and train them with the best equipment. What we ask of our people is complete loyalty and they get all the perks that come with their agreement. That means their choice of the best weapons."

He walked to a panel at one end of the hallway and pressed a series of numbers into a coded pad. "This is where the weapons are stored. We're two stories underground. If ever you find you've spent too much time down here practicing and sense the sun rising, there are cots in a room at the other end of the hall where you can sleep."

A panel door swung open and revealed the weapons. "Some of these are obviously meant to be used against those of the human world; others are for creatures like you met on the moors. Rogues are devils on Earth. I think you'll agree after having seen them. But there are vampires who are on the wrong side of the law and who *aren't* rogues. There are special weapons for them."

Morgan stepped back and took in dozens of side arms, assault rifles, swords, knives, and bladed weapons of all kinds. "I used a nine millimeter with a small revolver as a backup."

"We have anything you want here. Just remember that vampires—if they happen to be who you're after—can't be stopped by a bullet. So…what's your choice, Morgan?"

She stared. "Are you joking? Some of this stuff would cost me a year's salary."

"You came into this unwillingly. I think you're owed the choice of how to defend yourself, though I'll want a demonstration. Despite what your file says, I want to watch and see what you can do."

She wasn't daunted by his comment. She could use many of the automatic weapons displayed before her. "Are the blades used on…on rogues?"

He nodded. "As I told you before, aside from getting caught in the sun, wooden or silver stakes through the heart, decapitation, and fire are the best ways to take out another vampire. Bullets only piss us off. So what you don't know how to use, I'll show you."

Morgan looked over the display and got a very real sense of how deadly a vampire must be; how deadly *she* must be now. It was strange that she didn't feel evil or different. At least not as far as her psychology was concerned.

"Go on, Morgan. Choose anything."

She glanced at him, and his expression told her he was serious. If she wanted to survive, she had to be equally sincere. And she *did* want to survive. Last night on the moors had proven that. She'd fought and had felt fear.

She stretched out her hand and let it slide over several weapons. She felt the cold of steel and the warmth of wood and made choices that somehow seemed right.

"I'll take that semi-automatic there…and *that*."

Sean had to smile. "A nine millimeter and a crossbow?"

"Well, I don't know how good I'd be with a sword. I'd like to try my hand at a lot of these goodies. But *that* thing…" she stopped for a moment and nodded her head in approval. "I don't know. That crossbow just sort of…*does it* for me." She heard his low rumbling laugh and turned to him. It was at that moment Morgan realized he wasn't laughing *at* her, but in appreciation for her choice. His response temporarily incapacitated her communication skills. His beautiful, perfect smile was completely disarming.

"Excellent choice. You picked something you can hide under a long coat. It's light, can fire silver or wooden arrows, and is equally effective on humans *and* vampires. Better still…it's silent."

Somehow, his praise pleased her more than she wanted it to.

"I'll show you how to use a broadsword and you can carry one of those as well."

"Who uses the Claymore? I know what it is because I saw it in a movie once," Morgan relayed while pointing to a monstrously large, double-edged sword with a huge handle. She felt her eyes grow round as hubcaps. Such a weapon could only be wielded by a giant.

He burst out laughing again. "Wipe the doe-in-a-headlight look off your face, Morgan. You won't be swinging *that*."

"Who *could*?" she had to ask.

"A very good friend of mine. Play your cards right and I'll introduce you to him. For now, let's try out the nine millimeter." He pulled the weapon off the pegboard where it was displayed and opened a deep drawer at the bottom of the display unit.

"Here's where the ammo is kept. Any time you want to practice, just let me know. The keypad code is thirteen. I change it occasionally for security reasons. You'll sometimes see the guards practicing. So, if the ammo gets low, there's more stored down the hall. But you'll have to get the keys from me." He nodded in the direction of the locked ammo vault.

Morgan gently took the weapon from him and noted he handed it to her the way most cops would, with the handle facing toward her and the clip separate. She quickly stepped to the middle of the hall where she could see the targets hanging many yards away. For some reason, they looked a whole lot closer when she started to focus on them.

"You don't need the ear protection the way our human guards do, but if it makes you feel more comfortable, put it on."

Morgan saw the headgear lying on the counter in front of her but ignored it. She had to get used to this way of life. There wasn't any other choice. Again, she was reminded of the rogues and was determined to never die at their hands. She carefully loaded the weapon and turned her head toward Sean, waiting.

“What’s wrong?” he casually asked.

“I’m waiting for you to give me permission.”

Sean stepped up behind her. “Fire at will.”

Morgan aimed and pulled the trigger. She saw the sites on the gun as if they’d been painted with some glow-in-the-dark substance. The lighting in the firing lane was dim, but it didn’t matter. She still put fifteen rounds right through the center of the target and that was the best she’d ever done. She put the gun on the counter and turned to him when her last round hit the paper. Again, she was disarmed by the admiration in his steady gaze.

“*Excellent*. Want to try the crossbow?”

She physically stopped herself from jumping up and down in excitement, but not before he saw that first little hop.

Sean smirked. “Hold on *Robin Hood*…I’ll be right back.”

She eagerly waited for him to retrieve the weapon. Her hands almost itched to fire the small crossbow.

“Be careful with these,” Sean warned when he

returned. "Even a scratch from silver could injure you. If you hang onto them too long, they'll blister you. It's sort of like an allergy."

Morgan took them from him carefully and looked them over. She watched Sean walk to a panel on the wall where he flipped a switch. The paper targets were hoisted away and smaller, round targets replaced them. These, however, were some distance further away than she was used to. "Can you show me how to load this?"

***

Sean stood beside her and carefully exhibited how to maneuver the arrow into its notch, after pulling the firing lever back. "This particular model was designed by one of our people. Only we have them. So, don't let it get into anyone else's hands."

"Understood."

From the tone of her voice and the enthusiastic attitude she was displaying, Sean realized Morgan would take to training just as her files indicated. Her instructors had praised her as a dedicated individual and had decorated her for her work in the field, many times over. His initial reserve about her was quickly melting. She listened carefully and followed his instructions to the letter. The only low marks she'd ever received had to do with her tendency to seek perfection. That quality had its good and bad sides. However, it wasn't a severe problem as far as he was concerned.

He could almost sense her attempts to tap into her powers even without him showing her how. He watched her aim, fire, and land the arrow just a little to the left of the target's center.

"Damn!"

"What's wrong? That was an excellent shot," he told her.

She shook her head in denial. "It's not good enough. Two inches to the left might be the difference between coming home and *not* some night." She picked up another arrow, loaded it, and tried again.

That was her perfectionist side; the one he'd read about in her file. He saw the look of absolute concentration on her face and nodded in approval. For a full hour, he watched as she kept practicing. He was encouraged by her absolute insistence that the bow be conquered. Finally, however, he had to stop her.

"This is your first night, Morgan. You'll get the hang of it. And when you can load quickly *and* fire with accuracy, you'll have mastered the weapon. Why don't we try something else?" He saw her glare at the crossbow as it if was an enemy to be defeated. He had to take her arm to get her attention.

"Why don't we try something physical for a while?" he repeated.

"What?"

"In case you weren't aware of it, I've had access to your personnel file."

She lifted one shoulder and let it drop. "I assumed you could get your hands on it."

"Your record says you have a black belt in Kung Fu. I saw you use some skills on the rogues and I want to see more."

She slowly smiled. "Okay."

Sean motioned to her. "Follow me." He led her in a northerly direction and to a room off the hall. Neatly made cots were lined against one wall. A large workout floor had been built in the middle of the room. Weightlifting and boxing equipment also took up part of the space.

"The guys at my department would have loved this," Morgan commented in awe.

"Too bad they can't have something like it," Sean agreed. "It's like I said. We have the best equipment because we expect excellence from our people. If you want a piece of gear you don't see, tell Dani and she'll get it."

"I think you're jumping the gun. I haven't decided to

join this organization."

"Just look around and think of all this as an incentive," he replied as he took off his leather jacket, tossed it aside, and stepped into the middle of the open floor. When he saw her openly looking over his chest, it took everything he had to keep from laughing out loud. Indeed, he couldn't remember ever having such a good day down in the basement. There was something about the way Morgan openly exposed her emotions. But his sense of amiable mirth dissolved when he saw her staring straight into his eyes. The pure lust in them almost floored him.

"How big are your biceps?" she brazenly asked.

"I've never measured them."

"Shame," she responded.

He saw her gaze, with all its feral hunger, boldly wander over his entire body. In response, blood rushed to his groin. "Back to business, Morgan. Don't start something you can't finish."

His taunt was met with silence.

"What's wrong, Morgan? Not afraid of me, are you?" He finally saw her take a fighting stance opposite to where he stood. "It'll be Christmas soon. Attacking or not?" He continued to bait her, to get her mind off his body.

He watched her slowly circle with her hands in a guarded position and waited for any sign of attack. When he repeatedly lunged, she easily sidestepped each feint. He noted how she kept her gaze on him and appeared quite observant. She just wouldn't come near and take a shot, even when he left her an opening. He gave her more and more opportunities to hit him, and soon he became aware of time passing. His patience waned.

It finally occurred to him she *was* frightened. His senses picked it up as he kept making passes at her. She was probably wondering if he'd use his excessive strength inappropriately and take her head off by mistake. That was when he decided to press matters and force her into a position where she could see—even if she got hurt—she'd heal very quickly. Any pain wouldn't last long.

He was a bit disappointed at her lack of courage. All evening, she'd been holding up quite admirably. It seemed, once they'd stepped on this floor and she was faced with hand-to-hand combat, the bravery she'd displayed against the rogues melted. But maybe he was pushing too hard. Morgan had been through a lot in the last few days.

He took a deep breath and lunged at her again, with more force than necessary. His intent was to make her see she could take it.

He grabbed her upper arms and meant to pull her to the floor, but she didn't dodge; she didn't try to disengage his hands. Instead, she grabbed onto *his* upper arms as she sank gracefully toward the floor. She then rolled backwards and simultaneously planted her feet in his midsection. Inertia caused by her grip on his arms, her feet in his stomach, and her backward roll on the floor, forced his entire body to fly right over hers. He was now lying on his back and behind her. His poor, frightened little initiate quickly got to her feet again, sat on his chest, and hit him in the face with a nasty jab. He shook his head to get rid of the stars drifting before his eyes, blinked several times, and then stared up at her.

"I was wondering when you'd get tired of me dancing around you," Morgan said while smiling down at him.

He gazed up at her in confusion and raised his head slightly off the floor. "You were afraid. I sensed it and tried to get the fight over."

"Of course I was afraid. You're *huge*. Anybody with half a brain would be afraid of you."

Sean let the back of his head plop down on the floor again. "I read your fear wrong."

"Oh…I see," she nodded in understanding, "you thought I didn't have the nerve to fight at all."

He lifted the corners of his lips in an awkward smile. "Yes."

"Well, you know better now, don'tcha," she taunted and poked at his chest with the index finger of her right hand.

"Now that I know you'll use a larger opponent's weight against him, see if you can get out of this!" He quickly rolled over taking her with him. Morgan was beneath him and with her arms pinned down before she could utter another word. "Well, go on. Do your worst," he laughingly urged.

"You've got it," she told him as she quickly brought her knee up and contacted soft tissue.

Sean's breath left his body. He groaned in absolute anguish, placed his hands over his bruised testicles, and rolled to one side.

Immediately contrite, Morgan got up and knelt beside him. "God…I'm sorry, Sean! I just don't like guys pinning me down. It makes me feel threatened. And when I get scared—"

"I know," he gasped, "you go for the nuts!" As his agonizing pain gradually dissipated, he sat up. Morgan pushed his hair back and moved closer.

"I really *am* sorry."

"Only a fool fights an Irish woman," He remarked and slowly moved his hands from his groin. He saw her trying not to smile, but the glee in her eyes couldn't be contained.

"Oh, you think that whaling a man in the balls is funny, do you?" he merrily asked. "You did the same thing to that rogue. Something tells me you've done it before and you like it."

She put a hand over her mouth to hide her grin.

"All right, my lass. Sure 'n you owe me *this*."

Sean grabbed her by the shoulders, pulled her forward, and kissed her as hard as he could. He'd meant the contact to anger her and planned to let her go as soon as she pushed him away.

But something happened. Morgan *didn't* push him; she didn't get angry. For just an instant, she didn't respond at all. But when she did, her reaction was hot, raw, deep, and enticing. It reached him on all levels. He allowed his hands to wander over her body and felt her palms pressing against his chest.

He pulled her across his lap and ravaged her mouth with his. And Morgan gave as good as she got. Soft moans came from the back of her throat and nothing in the universe mattered but pleasing her.

It had been many years since that kind of passion gripped him. His entire body was on fire from the cells up. And Morgan still wasn't fighting it. She wasn't resisting a bit.

Chapter 5

Long lonely years spent in the service of *The Nightwatchers* crowded into Sean's mind. For over seven decades, he'd served the agency and never faltered in his devotion to its cause and goals. In the space of just a few days he found himself hiding this woman's initiation into vampirism, her uncle's participation in the event, and his friends' cooperation with a scheme that might not work. But the source of all the collusion was in his arms and he couldn't pull back. Her touch, her smell, and the very feel of her made him want something he thought he'd never have again. He ran his hands over her back and then plunged them into all that soft brown hair. He could imagine them making love so intensely that their cries would bring the roof down. And he wanted to be the one to give Morgan her first taste of vampire love. He wanted to see the light in her eyes as she experienced a female vampire's intense orgasm.

Sex between their kind was unbelievably fulfilling. It could last all night long. He was more than ready to show her a world of positions and caresses that could almost render her unconscious with pleasure. He molded her body to his and kissed her so deeply that she responded by pressing her full breasts against his chest. Her creamy skin was soft as an Irish breeze; it glowed in the dim light of the exercise room. If only the world would go away and leave them alone, they could do anything they wanted. And he knew she'd respond to any demand with passion, just as she was right now. Her tongue swirled against his, and he tasted the deep, rich sweetness of her lips.

But another time entered his mind. A promise he'd made so long ago filtered into the present and shot guilt into his heart. Or was it his fear of that time intruding into the moment?

He abruptly pulled away and stood, then turned to face a nearby wall. "Leave, Morgan. Leave while you can," he rasped.

"Sean, I know we've only known each other for a—"

"Just go," he interrupted and pointed to the exit without turning to face her.

Morgan did as he ordered.

He almost sensed her looking back at him before she finally departed.

After a long moment gaining his composure, he finally turned around and knelt on one knee. He tried to convince himself his response was due to overwork and long hours denying himself the pleasures of a female vampire. He'd had many since Simone had died. But none of them ever expected anything more than a night of rampant sex. That's all he could give and they knew it. Somehow, he thought Morgan would want more and it wasn't in him to deliver. This meant sharing his bed with her was impossible. And keeping her here any longer than necessary was also impossible. But he'd do what he always did when the loneliness closed in. He'd throw himself into work and purge the isolation from his system. She was only a woman, after all. Lust was nothing he couldn't handle.

He picked up a pair of boxing gloves, pulled them onto his hands, and proceeded to beat a nearby hanging bag until the stuffing came out.

***

Morgan spent the next few hours in her room. She showered and changed into one of the lovely dresses Dani had given her, in case the older woman showed up. It would be a kind gesture after all the friendship Danielle had shown. She convinced herself she only put the dress on for Dani's sake…no one else's. The older woman was as genuine as she'd always appeared. Morgan no longer doubted Dani's sincerity. As far as she was concerned, the two of them were now friends.

To take her mind off the many issues threatening to drive her insane, she sat at her desk and doodled aimlessly on a notepad. A knock sounded on the door and she answered woodenly. "Come in."

"Oh, you look lovely in that shade of green. It does wonders for your eyes," Dani gushed.

Morgan forced a smile. Dani was frank enough, but she was overdoing it a bit. "What's up?"

"I thought you and I could dine together. I was going to ask you to put on one of the nice outfits I brought back from Dublin, but there you are…all ready to go," she complimented. "You're simply radiant."

"Right back at you." Morgan eyed Dani's long black dress with suspicion. "I can't eat. At least, that's what I've been told."

Dani clasped her hands in front of her. "Well, I *can* and I don't like having my dinner alone. You could sit with me and have a drink, couldn't you?"

Morgan stood. "Why not?"

"Good. I'll just tell the staff to set places for three."

"Wait…I thought you didn't want to eat alone," Morgan said. "Why three?"

"I'm asking Sean to join us."

"I don't think that's a clever idea. When I left the basement, he acted like he wanted to be alone. Uh…he seemed intent on getting a good workout," she prevaricated.

"Well, I'll ask anyway. Perhaps he'll join us later. I'm just a bit tired of all this grim business governing our every waking moment," Dani told her. "We used to have the loveliest evenings here. We'd have other members of the agency join us to talk over problems or necessary interests. But we always ended up with long, leisurely meals. Very much like a family." She sighed. "All that seems like ages ago. We've all lost sight of the fact that we're coworkers who need to reach out to one another from time to time. We've let the horrors of the world make less of us, and it gives those who create the trouble so much more to gloat over," she reminisced with a shake of her head. "But you and I can at least sit down and talk after work is over. Since Patrick and I intend to be together, I think we could use the time to become closer. Don't you?"

Morgan slowly smiled and nodded. "Yeah, I guess that would be a promising idea. Especially since you'll be my aunt."

Dani burst out laughing. "That's right. I hadn't thought of it that way. If we can be a family, then so much the better. If Sean wants to join us, fine. If not," she shrugged, "it'll be his loss."

"I'll be down in a few minutes," Morgan promised as Dani walked toward the door.

"Just follow the sound of the music," Dani instructed. "I hope you don't mind, but I love to listen to music while I dine."

Morgan was still smiling when Danielle left the room. It was hard not to be happy when the older woman was around. Dani always tried to look at the positive side of everything. And if the elegant, lovely Englishwoman made her uncle happy, then she'd be euphoric for the both of them. They'd given up a great deal of their lives together so that Uncle Pat could see to *her* needs. It was their time now. Then it struck her that—other than for visits and holidays—there'd certainly be no place in their newly joined lives for a grown niece. They'd want their privacy and time to catch up on all they'd missed.

A sudden sense of loss hit her. Everything she loved was gone or changing. She swallowed the sudden lump in her throat and blinked back tears. Crying wouldn't accomplish anything. Dani would know if she succumbed to sorrow.

She lifted her chin, took a few deep breaths, and fought the urge to feel sorry for herself. More to the point, Sean…if he should make an appearance…might sense her sad mood. As far as their torrid scene in the gym went, she'd pretend it hadn't meant anything. In truth, all they'd done was kiss.

The situation suddenly seemed ridiculous. How many

women could say they'd been attracted to a gorgeous vampire after knocking his nuts between his ears? When she thought of the situation this way, her Irish American humor got the better of her and she was actually chuckling by the time she made her way downstairs.

She did as instructed and followed the sound of soft, Celtic harp music into a sumptuous living room. Dani stood by an open door leading to a garden. Colorful flowers were clearly visible outside, and their fragrance wafted throughout the space. The night couldn't hide their presence or their hues from her.

"This is beautiful," Morgan said as she held out her hands to encompass the sage green walls, the tapestry-covered, overstuffed chairs, and the cherry coffee table. The ceiling, she noted, was high and adorned with carved white woodwork in Celtic designs. The room was regally appointed and exquisitely tasteful.

In the center of the adjoining room, a long cherrywood

dining table shone under the light of a crystal chandelier. Someone had laid out a single setting for one diner, complete with a gleaming white plate on an Irish linen placemat. Irish crystal wine glasses had been placed in front of two high-back chairs that could have graced any medieval castle.

"Who decorated all this?" Morgan asked in a hushed and overwhelmed tone.

"That would be me," Dani modestly admitted, as she handed Morgan a glass of blood. "I tried to give it a subtle medieval ambiance while obviously bringing the lighting up to date."

"From clothes to homes, your taste is magnificent," Morgan told her. "I feel like royalty."

"You certainly look it, dear. I only wish your uncle were here to share this evening."

Morgan put her hand on Dani's arm. "He'll be here before you know it. And something tells me he'll only have eyes for you."

She'd long since tossed aside the idea of using Dani to get free. The woman was soon to be a family member and, for Pat's sake, she was very glad. Her uncle could have done much worse for himself.

When footsteps sounded in the hall, they turned to see a very tall, masculine presence enter the room.

***

Sean didn't want to join the women after what happened in the gym. His emotions were still reeling over a romantic interlude that should never have taken place. However, staying in his room would only hurt Dani's feelings, and Morgan might conclude that he couldn't handle being near her. He had to act as if their encounter was nothing more than a stimulating moment brought on by mutual loneliness. It was just a kiss.

He walked to a sideboard and poured himself a glass of blood. One of the maids entered the dining room and set the table with food for Dani and more blood for Morgan and himself. While seeing the dark fluid in Irish crystal didn't make it taste richer, one could easily mistake it for wine. He knew Dani wasn't put off by his drinking the stuff, but it was polite not to make it obvious. Good Irish crystal could make sludge look wonderful.

Morgan perched her slender frame on the arm of an overstuffed chair. They politely exchanged a nod but nothing more. He smiled at Dani, made civil conversation with her, and sensed Morgan staring a hole through his back. He'd taken pains *not* to dress with any concern for Morgan's opinion, but to please Dani. His pants and boots were still black leather, but the black silk shirt he wore was left open since it was an artist style. Dani had told him once that he looked like a highwayman in this get-up. She'd also said she'd loved it since it gave him a rakish look. The comment had produced amusing conversation long into the night. The memory of that happy evening was the reason he wore the clothes, certainly not for anyone *else's* sake.

When the maid left and Dani moved to the table, Sean held her chair out and then did the same for Morgan. Despite their living in a world where such gestures could be considered misogynistic, and certainly *not* politically correct, he still maintained the manners he'd been taught as a child. But doing so made him notice how low the back of Morgan's dark green dress plunged and how high the halter-top lifted her breasts. The fabric flowed over her body and legs in such an intimate way that he found himself wishing she'd stand up. His mouth went dry, he felt flushed, though of course that was impossible. Vampires simply did not *flush*. Still...images of picking Morgan up in his arms and carrying her to his room flooded his brain. *What the shaggin' hell is wrong with me?*

He tried—*God knew how he tried*—to look at anything besides her beautiful face, her sparkling green eyes, and the way her full red lips curved when she presented a perfect, white smile. A breeze from the garden lifted her long hair from her shoulders as he took his seat. He gripped the arms of his chair so no one would see his hands shaking. It actually

angered him that Morgan could look so unconcerned while *he* was in danger of over-heating. He dared a glance in her direction, then did a double take when he saw her eyeing Dani's roast beef and potatoes. There was a wistful, softness in her gaze. But then she looked away and put red-tipped, slender fingers to her lips as if the very sight of food were nauseating. The ability to view it with dispassion would come. He kept his gaze on her long enough to make sure she drank her drink. Only doing so would stem her queasiness.

He had to make conversation. The women were the only ones talking at the moment, and Dani would certainly notice if he didn't say *something*. She knew him better than anyone in the household. But all the angels in heaven could never explain why he directed his casual query to the person he'd been trying to ignore.

"So, Morgan…what would you most like to learn about vampirism?"

"I think I'd like to learn that shapeshifting thing," she readily replied.

He shook his head. "You're not ready. Not yet."

Dani sipped her wine and said, "I've been told it's one of the hardest undertakings for vampires. Training for it usually comes last."

Morgan wouldn't be put off. "How is it done?"

"Our scientists have never figured it out," Sean explained. "It's a mind-over-matter issue. One simply thinks of the animal then changes into it."

"Bats? Wolves?" Morgan questioned.

No matter how hard he tried, he couldn't fight Morgan's open charm. The candid intelligence in her eyes warmed him again, the way it had down in the basement. "Yes to both animals. But don't try it on your own. Without the proper focus, you'll only give yourself a headache," he warned. "I'll teach you when I think you're ready.

"When will that be?" she asked, then leaned forward

and chewed on her lower lip in expectation.

Dani began to chuckle.

Sean tried not to smile. Morgan's face was lit with enthusiasm. It was so pure, wonderful, and strong that those around her were infected. He relaxed, stared at her, and shook his head. She was exactly like an eager kid who kept asking *are we there yet.*

Morgan grinned. "I won't let this go."

"I know you won't, you little—" he stopped and cleared his throat when he saw Dani glancing between him and Morgan with a *what's going on between you two* expression pasted on her face. He decided to change the subject entirely, hoping an honest comment about Morgan's gown would divert Dani's tabloid-like attention.

"That dress is fantastic."

"It's Dani's gift," Morgan announced as she smoothed out the dark green material on her lap. "Her taste is excellent."

"But it's the body filling it that's intriguing," Dani

remarked. "Don't you agree, Sean?"

He fixed is gaze on Morgan and had to tell the unconditional truth. "I do." He saw his *Lady Robin Hood* finally lower her eyes and sip her blood. Sadly, she seemed to lose her sprightly eagerness. The rest of the conversation was ordinary by comparison.

Dani put her napkin down a half hour later, glanced at her companions and suggested. "The meal was wonderful, but the night is young for those who live in it. Why don't we change the music? I'd love to dance. It's been such a long time."

Morgan rallied. "I love to dance, too."

Sean stood as the women did, then followed them into the living room.

Dani walked to an entertainment center, shut off the harp music, made her choice and turned the volume up. "Anyone up for a waltz?" she gaily asked.

"You always wear me out, Dani," Sean joked.

"Who said anything about taking a turn with *you?*" Dani teased and then playfully skipped over to Morgan.

Sean snickered when the two women adoringly gazed into each other's eyes, moved cheek to cheek, and made one round of the room to the music. He crossed his arms over his chest and waited for them to acknowledge his presence. Dani finally did so by waltzing Morgan over to his location and shoving the younger woman at him. Morgan was still smirking at Dani's silliness when she was pushed forward.

Sean looked her over before moving an inch. He'd been right. The shimmering fabric of her dress could only be appreciated when the wearer was standing upright. Only then could a person enjoy the full length of her toned body.

He moved his palm to the small of her back, pulled her body closer, and felt her stiffen. The glee in her gaze turned to heat when she looked up at him. Sean knew their roles had somehow reversed. *She* was now the one being affected by *him*. "Relax," he whispered.

"I…I'm trying."

Sean inhaled the wonderful lemon scent that was Morgan, and every nuance of their kiss came tumbling back. Her body melded to his as she finally unwound. They moved fluidly around the floor, and he kept his gaze only on her eyes. There was confusion in her expression, but not aversion. He sensed her uncertainty but wanted to encourage her to enjoy the dancing.

As his fingers stroked the small of her back, she pressed her breasts against him. A voice in his head kept repeating one phrase over and over. *She's exquisite.* Another, more prudent warning echoed for him to *remain uninvolved.*

As soon as the song finished, they moved apart and he immediately felt the loss of her nearness. Dani stood to take a turn and he found himself needing his friend close so his ardor would cool. His trusted assistant was the calm versus Morgan's tempest. "Come on, Dani. It's been a long time," he comfortably said as she took Morgan's place.

When the music ended and Sean led Dani to a nearby chair, he also offered her a glass of wine as she sat. When he glanced at Morgan, something in her face alerted him. She was staring into the distance and contemplating some subject that clouded her expression.

"Morgan, I've been choosing all the music. Why don't you go play something *you* like," Dani suggested.

Morgan mechanically nodded and got up to look over a collection of old vinyl records.

The song she chose to play could only have been picked by coincidence, but it still made Sean freeze on the spot.

I'll Be Seeing You, as sung by Dinah Shore, was haunting in its simplicity and message. It had *always* made him feel as though a sliver of ice was being rammed straight through his heart. He hadn't heard the particular tune in decades because everyone in the entire compound knew *not* to play it around him. It was his and Simone's song.

He actually sensed Dani stiffening and knew she was waiting to see what he'd do. Before she could contact her restraining hand, he uttered a venomous remark, directed straight at Morgan. He did this while simultaneously racing to the music console to remove the offensive song.

"Never play that song again. *Never*!" he furiously commanded as he sat the disc on the top of the machine and stared at it. *"Get it out of this house!"*

He turned to find the two women staring at him. Dani's face was filled with pity and empathy. Morgan was glaring at him as if he'd lost his mind.

Sean couldn't contain the emotions welling in him. He tossed a music chair to one side and stormed out. The only respite for him now was in the privacy of his bedroom.

After he'd gone, there was a very long moment of intense silence.

Dani held out one hand in supplication and walked toward Morgan. "I'm so sorry. This is my fault."

"What *fault*?" Morgan slowly queried. "What the hell did I do?"

"You don't understand. That record was one I took from attic storage. When I was packing your belongings back in LA, I saw that you had the exact same CD version of the album, in your apartment. It was titled *Old Tunes from the War.* I thought of it and…well…never mind what I thought," she slowly responded. "The point is, I was ordered to destroy the record a long time ago. If Sean had known it was even on the premises, he'd have thrown it in the fireplace."

"No wonder I recognized the music," Morgan murmured. "It *was* a song I used to listen to. But I still don't understand what made Sean go thermonuclear!"

"I've said all I should. It's his business and I just can't say more. At least not until he feels compelled to tell you."

Morgan looked at the record now sitting on the top of the old and expensive record player. "Maybe you'd better get rid of it."

She handed the offending music to Dani, then turned to leave.

"I'd hoped we'd have a nice evening together," Dani murmured. "Like it used to be."

Morgan hesitated, looked over her shoulder at Dani, and softly said, "I'll dine with you anytime you like. If *His Highness* doesn't approve, he can stay in his damned room. We'll turn on the music and dance with each other until our shoes fall off. Who needs a man?"

Dani tearfully smiled.

Morgan quietly left the room.

***

An hour before sunrise, Sean was still sitting in the chair behind his desk, trying to rid himself of memories. How could he have forgotten Simone's death? And why, with hundreds of songs to choose from, had Morgan chosen that particular one? Why hadn't Dani destroyed it, as he'd asked?

He could almost believe that Morgan had done it on

purpose except she couldn't know about his past. He was sure Dani would never reveal such an intimate part of his personal life. He cast his gaze at his closed bedroom door, knowing Morgan had retreated to her room some time earlier. He got up, paced for a few minutes, then left his room and marched down the hall toward her door. Knocking harder than he meant to and about to apologize for having done so, his anger was renewed by Morgan's leisurely response.

When she finally opened the door, he walked in without waiting for her invitation.

"Why don't you come in," she sarcastically remarked after he pushed past her. She shut the door and crossed her arms over her robed chest. "Was there something you wanted in particular, or are you pissed about something *else*?"

He rounded on her and walked to within a few inches of where she stood. "I was coming to apologize for the way I acted, but I need to know why you chose that *particular* song."

"Clearly, you've been fuming over this for hours and

aren't going to give it a rest." She paused. "I like music from that era. The CD of the same vinyl album was from a collection of mine. Dani saw it in my apartment and thought hearing it would make me relax. If I'd known you didn't like it, I certainly wouldn't have played the damned song."

He looked into her eyes and knew she was telling the absolute truth, but it was too much of a coincidence. Sean couldn't let the matter go. "Why? Why do you like music from the Thirties and Forties?"

She pushed her hair back with one hand. "I don't know…what difference does it make? I-I suppose it's because it was a very romantic era. People were filled with a common goal to fight for a worthy cause. They stuck together more back then than they do now. The music evokes patriotism and hope." She shrugged. "Hell, Sean, I just like it. Lots of people do, you know."

"There was nothing romantic about that time. And while people might have wanted to fight for a cause, they suffered for it as well. You can't begin to imagine the horror wrought during those years." He turned away and walked to a far corner of the room. A small desk halted his retreat from her stimulating presence.

"How old are you, Sean?"

For a long moment, he didn't speak. "I was born in 1909."

"Can I ask where?"

He took a deep breath before responding. "It was a small fishing village on the northern coast. The name of it was Beag Baile. It doesn't even exist anymore. There were only a few families living in the area back then. The name literally means *small town*." Sean took a deep breath as many memories returned and begged to be voiced. "My father was a fisherman. I always remember him as being very big, with a huge smile on his face. My mother…she baked the best soda bread heaven ever put on an Irish table. And she was flamin' beautiful." Something was making him ramble, but he had to get his thoughts out.

Morgan moved closer.

"I died on the morning of December 16, 1944. The day *The Battle of the Bulge* began."

She swallowed hard before asking, "H-How did you become a vampire?"

"I got shot during a covert operation. A *Nightwatcher* vampire was present when I was brought to an Allied field hospital. Since I was a human member of the organization, I got the choice of becoming a vampire or dying."

"I-I'm sorry. It must have been hell back then. That music I played probably reminded you of a lot of things you'd rather have forgotten."

"I never forgot anything. The music just made me..." he left the sentence unfinished.

Morgan walked forward and put a hand in the middle of his back. "I won't ever play it again. I'm sorry, Sean. It's evoking some very bad memories."

"It's not your fault. You didn't know. People who weren't there could never really understand. Reading about it in a book or seeing it in a movie or in a documentary doesn't put you where you could smell it and feel the cold or the terror. There were thousands all over Europe who lost their homes. They survived for years on rations and waited for the postman to bring letters about loved ones they'd never see again. Women lost husbands, brothers, and entire families. Men lost wives, sisters, and a future generation of mothers. Children were orphaned and the good people of the world struggled on while Hitler and his brutish cowards killed whoever got in their way. Innocent people died along with the guilty. No one was spared," he expounded.

Morgan pulled her robe closer and quietly listened.

"I began as a code analyst in Bletchley Park. Have you heard of it?"

"Yes," Morgan softly replied. "It's where some special equipment was placed for the Allies to filch out enemy communication, wasn't it?"

He nodded. "As a boy, I had an affinity for languages, especially German. By the time the war broke out, I was teaching in a boy's school in Dublin. Though Ireland remained neutral during the war, many of my countrymen fought against Hitler anyway. Like them, I volunteered my services and joined an Irish infantry unit called the *Third Celtic Horse Guard*. We were assigned to fight with an American unit." He sighed and passed a hand over the back of his neck. "Because of my translation abilities, I was immediately put in a position where I could decode German messages. Soon, agents of *The Nightwatchers* approached me and indoctrinated me into what was secretly known as *Unit Thirteen*."

"What's that?"

"It was one of several descriptors we sometimes used for operations back then. So that no one would know the actual name of the organization," he explained. "We came and went without questions being asked, much as we do today.

My communication skill rapidly got me advanced into some highly clandestine operations." He fell silent, remembering those days vividly.

"Go on," Morgan softly prompted. "What happened?"

Sean ran both hands through his hair and continued. It was like someone opened a gate and he couldn't close it. Everything had to come out. "Eventually, I was transferred to Belgium. I was teamed with a German national who, as a vampire, was giving the Allies information on where enemy troops were moving. Later, a French agent was teamed with us. She dealt with the Nazis in her homeland. And with her being a vampire as well as my German friend, we made quite a team…Skord, Simone and me," he said as Morgan stood and listened. "Skord and Simone ferreted out the locations of the troops by night. I took the information they got back to headquarters by day. We got so used to what we were doing…I don't think any of us realized how vulnerable we were."

"You were running on pure nerve. It's like what I felt when I was a cop," Morgan relayed.

"Yes. I think the power we felt was one of the things that kept us at it. Day after day, night after night. The three of us knew no fear. We felt we could conquer the enemy ourselves and toast our victories." He briefly closed his eyes before going on. "You know…back then it never occurred to me that vampires could be vulnerable. I never thought to ask Skord why one of them—as stealthy and deadly as they are—couldn't have gotten to Hitler and taken him out."

Morgan simply stared fixedly at him.

Sean glanced down at the floor for a moment. "Hell…it would have been an unfair question. Hitler's trusted staff tried to kill him and couldn't. I don't know how I ever thought a stranger, vampire *or* human, could get near that madman…not as paranoid as he and his henchmen were." He clenched his hands, and then relaxed them. "I-I guess the point I'm trying to make is…everyone was dying all around us, and we somehow got the idea nothing could hurt us. We thought ourselves invincible. The truth was," he quietly continued, "we were living on borrowed time. Sooner or later, one or all of us were bound to make the last sacrifice. The circumstances were just too dangerous. Vampire or human…exposure to sunlight or a bullet…we were all vulnerable."

"Keep going, Sean. I'd really like to hear this. I want to know what you felt. Who were you then? Who were these other people…your friends?"

"Back then, my surname was Murphy. Skord's last name was Proust. And Simone...her surname name was Marchant. She and I eventually posed as newlyweds," Sean explained and he gazed into the distance for a moment. "It was easy for Skord and me to get access to areas off limits. All we had to do was wear German uniforms or civilian clothing and use forged paperwork. Simone could talk to shopkeepers and village women. She had a knack for putting them at ease, and Skord was such a formidable presence that no one dared question him." Sean frowned due to memories flooding through his brain. "It seemed there was no information we couldn't get our hands on." He paused and then asked, "Do you know the old phrase, *familiarity breeds contempt*?"

"Yes," she gently agreed. "I know what it means."

"One night we were deep in German territory, scouting out bombing locations for the Allies. We came upon some people moving about in a wooded area. It was just a few miles west of a Nazi camp," he said in a mechanical voice. "I waited by our car for signs of German troops. Skord and Simone went into the woods to see what they could. But it wasn't soldiers they found there. It was a couple of Jesuit nuns, a downed British pilot and some refugee children the nuns were hiding from the Nazis."

"*My God*," Morgan uttered while shaking her head.

The look of utter sincerity in her lovely eyes kept him going. He had to tell the rest of it. "When they heard us approach, the adults in the group went scurrying about the woods, trying to get the children to hide. It took Skord and Simone two hours to track them all down and explain we were no threat." He clenched his hands. "I even had to talk to the pilot and give the man some ammunition before he'd believe us. That was when he told me Jewish, Romanian and Polish children, as well as Catholics, were routinely rounded up by the Germans and sent to what we thought were work camps." Sean bitterly snorted. "That was a kinder name for them."

"Did you get the children and everyone else out?" Morgan desperately asked.

Sean continued without giving her a direct answer. "I had to see what the British officer was talking about when he referred to the camps with such horror. Had I known…" his voice trailed away for a moment, but then he picked up the story again. "Simone stayed behind with the group while Skord and I traveled to one of the nearest compounds. We had to see for ourselves if what the pilot said was true. Even Skord couldn't believe it."

"It was Buchenwald," Morgan whispered when she remember Sean mentioning the name.

He slowly nodded. "We got close enough to get a good look. Skord was able to shapeshift and get even closer. When he came back, there was this terrible expression on his face. An expression that I'd never seen before. When he told me what the Nazis were doing there, we knew we had to get those children away and get back to headquarters as soon as possible. Even then I didn't want to believe what Skord told me, but no one could make up something like he described. It's not possible for someone to just imagine what I smelled and what he saw."

Morgan put her hands to her face and Sean saw her struggling not to cry.

Still, he couldn't stop. For some reason there was no way he could now. He put his hands on her shoulders. "That was when everything started to go wrong. We'd got so used to patting ourselves on the backs for our ingenuity. We weren't prepared for what happened," he elaborated. "We made mistakes. And it cost us. It cost…" he stopped, momentarily unable to say words that had to come out.

Morgan stood in front of him and waited. He stared at her. From the look in her eyes, he knew the horror and the revulsion he was instilling.

"Tell me. *Please,* Sean."

Chapter 6

"A German patrol stopped Skord and me when we were on our way back to the woods. They weren't sure about our travel documents, so they asked us to wait until they could confirm them. We…we *had* to kill them," Sean sadly admitted. "There was no other choice. But one of the soldiers was able to fire his rifle before we could get to him. The sound of it alerted every patrol in the area." He put one hand on his chest as though he could still feel his heart beating as hard as it was that day. "We grabbed their weapons and the vehicle they'd been using and got back to the woods as quick as we could."

"Sean…the kids?"

"It was only an hour before sunrise and I knew Skord and Simone would have to find a hollowed-out tree or a cave…or they'd have to dig themselves into the ground when the sun came up," he told her while speaking faster now.

"That only left me and the pilot to do any fighting. With the children at risk, we decided not to make a stand but to run for it. Still, no matter what we did, the Germans were on us every step of the way."

Morgan gripped the front of his shirt.

"We managed to lose them only ten minutes before sunrise. By that time both our vehicles were almost out of fuel."

"How far from Allied lines were you?" she quickly asked.

"Another two days. But we had to keep going. We couldn't let those children go to…and that was if the soldiers didn't shoot them on the spot. I *know* they would have killed the British officer and the nuns."

"What happened next, Sean?" Morgan demanded. "I have to know—"

"We ditched our transportation and hoped the Germans wouldn't find where we put the cars. In the woods, there were many places to conceal ourselves," Sean recalled as he nodded. "By the time the sun came up, Skord and Simone were well hidden. I told the nuns and the British officer that Skord and Simone were scouting ahead. We hid the children, I fed them what rations we had, and we dug in for the day. We could hear the German patrols searching for us." He lifted his head slightly. "The children never made a single sound. The youngest was about five…the oldest around fifteen. They sensed they were in danger and had to keep quiet."

"*Sweet Mother of God*! I never imagined it was so horrible," Morgan whispered. "I never understood..."

Sean blundered on, needing to get through the story so badly that he actually felt pain in his chest. "By that night, Skord and Simone were back from hiding. We couldn't take even the slightest chance that someone would hear the noise from the cars, so we trudged deeper into the woods without transportation. All through the night and into the next, we carried the children who were too small and tired. Even the bigger children carried the smaller ones. And we almost made it, Morgan! We almost got them to safety." He started to shake, then tears blurred his vision. "Only a few miles from the front, we got caught in some heavy ordnance from the German side. There was an explosion…three of the children…along with one of the nuns…and…Simone. They were killed," he haltingly blurted as he stared straight into Morgan's eyes. "Remember I told you how vampires could be killed? Do you recall me saying decapitation was one of the ways? "

"Sean no!" she choked out, then looped her arms around his shoulders and leaned her head against his chest.

"We finally got the rest of the group back across Allied lines." Sean swallowed hard, blinked back tears and tried to finish. "Years later the British officer married, had a child and divorced. That man then joined the organization." He took a deep breath and tried to speak coherently. The story was so near being completed. The last words had to be spoken so

Morgan understood. "That pilot…was Dani's father. She was born quite late in his life, but he loved her terribly. He even recruited her into the organization and sent her to me. She was twenty-three when I first met her."

"She's been with you for so long?" Morgan murmured very quietly.

"She's in her fifties now. And knowing Danielle wouldn't be here but for Skord and me, I keep thinking of those dead children and the kids *they* may have had; the lives they might have led."

By now, the tears he'd tried to hold back wouldn't be contained. "I was so in love with Simone," he whispered. "She was going to initiate me into vampirism. We planned to be together forever and that song you played was our favorite." He kindly broke the embrace, cupped her cheeks with his hands, and stared into her eyes. "Don't ever think you can't be destroyed. Never take your powers for granted and learn everything you can about surviving. Do you understand?" He shook her gently. "Swear you'll be careful, Morgan. *Swear it*!"

She nodded but said nothing more.

He pulled her against his chest again, held her for only an instant and then let her go again.

"Sean, don't leave," she blurted. "Stay with me for the rest of the night."

"Didn't you get what I just told you? You don't mix business with pleasure!" he adamantly insisted. "It's a rule you'd better learn if you plan on joining the agency." He backed away from her.

"Sean, you must have had other women. That was decades ago and a man like you—"

"Yes, I've had *many* women since then. I'm not a damned saint. I have needs. But the lovers I choose are always vampires, and all of them are looking for a man whose stamina can match their own. They don't know this agency exists. As far as they're concerned, I'm just another independent male of our species who's looking for entertainment. They never want more from me than a night of very unusual sex; anything keeping them from being bored out of their minds for the rest of eternity," he soberly told her.

"You won't try to have anything more?" she quietly asked. "I mean…how can you keep putting the past ahead of your future? I'd think, after seeing what you have, you'd *want* to find the joy in life. Surely your job isn't all there is?"

"It's all there is for me. It *has* to be. And I suggest you learn from my mistakes. Don't get permanently involved with anyone if you're going to join this organization. It doesn't pay!"

Morgan lifted her chin and said, "I don't think you have to worry about it."

Sean shook his head as if doing so could help him get control of his emotions. "I've…I've talked too much. I should leave before the sun comes up," he said without waiting for a response.

He would have exited the room but stopped when a

note on her desk caught his attention. "What's this?" he asked.

"None of your business. I was just fooling around," Morgan assured as she tried to snatch the paper away from him.

Sean stepped back so she'd quit grabbing for the note. "Every form of communication in this compound is approved by me. Otherwise it's destroyed," he sternly instructed. "If you were writing to someone, I'll need to know who. None of your American friends can know you're alive, Morgan! I shouldn't need to say so."

"I wasn't writing to anybody. It's nothing." She reached for the paper again, but Sean tactfully pushed her back and began to scan it.

He tried not to respond at all when he saw the cartoon drawing at the top of the page. A ridiculous looking bat had just flown into a brick wall and its eyes were crossed in presumed pain. The caption read, *Never fly when you can walk.* But the rest of the words on the page puzzled him. It read like a shopping list.

Chocolate, beer, pizza, spaghetti, garlic bread, ice cream, popcorn, chocolate, Mexican food, fresh oranges, Irish whiskey, nachos, potatoes with gravy, bar-b-que, thick steaks with little mushrooms, chocolate…

Sean blinked in confusion. The list went on and on. Chocolate was itemized no less than fifteen times. *"What the hell is this?"*

"I told you, it's *nothing*." She looked away and shifted her weight from one foot to the other.

He sensed her embarrassment, looked at the scrawled writing again and back at Morgan. Then it dawned on him. These were things she liked and couldn't ever have again. He slowly handed the paper back. "Here, you can have it."

"Never mind. Just shred it. It's not worth saving."

He simply nodded, pocketed the note, and walked toward the door. "It's almost sunrise. Rest well, Morgan. I…I didn't mean to come in here and unload on you. I apologize. I need to work on my self-control."

She tucked a strand of hair behind her ear and smiled at him. "It's okay. Everybody needs somebody to talk to, sooner or later. And I'm glad you told me. I understand a lot now."

He didn't stay to find out exactly what the last statement meant. He walked back to his room, undressed, and felt the instinctive lethargy the sunrise always brought. It was like being called to hibernate.

Instead of leaving the note in the shredding bin, he got into bed and looked it over once more. Then, he carefully folded it, opened the drawer to his nightstand, and stuck it in his mother's old jewelry chest. There wasn't anything of real value in the small box, but what he wanted from his past was all there—along with Morgan's list.

***

For the next five weeks, Sean trained Morgan and pushed her harder than he'd ever worked anyone. But rather than complain, she took up every challenge and exceeded all the goals he set for her. There wasn't a repeat of the hot scenario in the gym. He kept himself tightly reined and wouldn't let her presence get under his skin. But it began to irritate *him* that Morgan never mentioned their kiss or so much as made a single personal comment.

Wasn't she doing exactly as he'd asked? Wasn't she keeping everything totally professional and by the book?

When he joined her and Danielle for their continued evenings together, Morgan would come down the stairs like some Celtic goddess in a new outfit more beautiful than the last. And while she and Dani got closer, Morgan seemed more than ready to distance herself from *him* and Greenwood forever.

Finally, he knew what he had to do. As he rose from sleep on a late summer evening, he walked to Morgan's room, knocked on the door and waited. She responded in tight-fitting black leather and he almost changed his mind about his decision.

"Instead of training, I thought we'd leave the compound and go into Dublin tonight." Her beaming smile didn't make what he was doing any easier.

"Are you going to teach me to shapeshift?"

"No. There's someone I want you to meet. You might remember me mentioning him when I told you about the war. His name is Skord Shorner."

"I'll get my coat."

Just like that. She didn't ask any questions or seem the least bit concerned that rogues might still be outside the compound waiting for them. Her nonchalance bothered him even though he knew she was a good fighter. When she walked out the door and would have started down the hall, he gently took her upper arm and stopped her. "Stay close to me, understand? We won't be leaving without taking a trip to the armory first."

"Sure. I expected that." She pulled on some black

leather gloves and smoothed back the hair which perpetually escaped her ponytail.

He wanted to shake her. She should be more attentive to her safety. Instead, Morgan was treating the entire situation like it was a Sunday picnic. "You do realize those rogues could be near?"

"Yeah. But I'm a lot better prepared than the last time. Besides, I've gotta do this. Nice as this place is, I'm sick of being cooped up here."

He expelled a long breath as she walked down the hall and pushed the elevator button.

From the basement armory, they took what he deemed necessary in the way of defense. Then he led her back into the elevator. Once they were on the first floor, he took her toward the back of the house and out the kitchen door. "It's a clear night. May as well use my bike."

Morgan followed him to the back of the property, where there was an old carriage house. Sean pushed a button, a garage door opened and she gasped at the huge, custom-built American motorcycle gleaming in front of her. There were rows of racked helmets lined up near the bike, in assorted styles and hues.

"Oh, I've gotta drive this." She reached out and stroked the chrome as if it were precious.

"Not on your life!" he immediately responded. "No one…and I mean *no one*… touches my bike. Besides, I don't remember anything in your file saying you've had experience with them."

She grinned. "It wouldn't be in any file. I dated a couple of motorcycle cops and they let me ride their bikes all the time. Something like that isn't put in your work record." She quickly got back to the subject at hand. "Come on, Sean. I'm a good driver, and I'll be careful."

"No. Besides, you haven't got any ID."

"You've had time to make me a hundred IDs by now," Morgan complained.

"No, there's a lot that goes into it. We have to build you a very detailed, fake profile so nothing can be traced back to us. If the Gardai pulled you over, what would you show them?" he sternly asked while referring to Ireland police who worked the area. "I doubt he or she would let the lack of a permit go unnoticed even for your pretty smile. Besides, you didn't need an ID since you couldn't leave the property anyhow," he asserted. "Now…get on. And don't forget to wear a helmet."

"Why would we wear helmets? We're vampires."

He stared at her. "We obey the local laws and they require the use of helmets. We don't draw attention to ourselves if we can help it, and as I've just stated, you don't have identification. If we get pulled over right now, you could end up in jail. I don't want to explain such an occurrence to Fergus MacArtan when wearing a damned helmet would have prevented any problems."

Morgan rolled her eyes and got on the bike after he did.

"What if someone wants to check my passport? I don't have that *either* and I'm not Irish."

"If we encounter anyone asking for *any* kind of ID, you let me handle it," he slowly uttered in frustration. "These incidents have happened before; I know what to do. *Understand*?"

"Yes sir," she sarcastically shot back. "By the way, whatever cologne you're wearing…"

"Yes?"

"It smells fantastic," she smilingly provided.

He didn't miss the soft sigh or the way she tightened her grip around his waist. For a moment, Sean wanted to take her hands and wrap them even tighter around his body. He had to keep his wits and his distance. There simply wasn't any room in his life for entanglements. And with Morgan, the romantic interludes they could share might all too easily develop into something neither of them needed. He pulled on his helmet after making sure she had strapped hers on, then started the bike. He drove it out onto the service road and along the side driveway to the front. When the gates automatically opened, he pulled out onto the road and stopped for a moment.

"What's wrong?" Morgan asked.

"Do you sense anything different? Anyone near who doesn't feel natural to you?"

Morgan sat up straight and looked out into the hills. "I don't think there's anything out there."

"You don't *think* or you're *sure*?" he angrily prodded.

"There's nothing there, Sean."

He heard the irritation in her voice, but it didn't matter. Morgan had to keep her wits about her and learn to sense others of their kind from a distance. As time went on, she'd become experienced in this life, her powers would grow. Right now, only the most careful vigilance would keep her safe. For that reason, he knew he was doing the right thing by introducing her to his best friend. "Hang on."

***

Morgan did as he ordered and couldn't help feeling a damned site more liberated. If she'd stayed at Greenwood one more day, without the freedom of even a walk on the hillsides, she'd have gone crazy. The only thing that actually kept her from going over the wall again was the thought of running into those hideous rogues. Sure, she could take care of herself if the odds were fair. But those who liked fighting rarely did so fairly. That's why she'd learned early on to kick men where they lived and drop even the biggest foe quickly. In the course of her former work, if brawn weren't accompanied by brains, someone could die.

A lot of good cops died by thinking they could handle anything and not calling for backup. She surmised this line of work was pretty much the same. Sean was one of those men who didn't want to work with anyone. That bothered her on various levels. First, he was perfectly aware of the dangers but was exposing himself by not having a partner; at least none she knew about. Second, the thought of something happening to him was chilling. After everything he'd been through, Sean deserved some kind of peaceful life; at least some semblance of a safer one from time to time. But Danielle said he never took vacations, rarely went out with coworkers, or took up hobbies to take his mind off what he did. Morgan had seen cops like that. They got what was known as tunnel vision and never saw the big picture that was life. All they knew, ate, breathed, or slept was their work. It had the net effect of making them dangerous on duty.

Cops like that were sometimes too judgmental, and they got so overzealous that their actions could be unpredictable. Her heart ached for a man who deserved better than to live his life so consumed by the past that he couldn't look to the future or simple joys in everyday existence. Because of all this, Morgan couldn't be around him. She couldn't let herself get too close to a man who allowed a cloud of death to cast shadows over everything he did; even to the extent that he couldn't listen to a certain kind of music without feeling pain.

***

The miles flew by as Sean expertly maneuvered the big bike through the country lanes and into the city. Less than ten minutes after reaching Dublin, he found a good parking spot, pulled into it and shut off the engine. "This is it," he nodded toward a building and the familiar vampire guard watching the back door. A bright green neon sign hung over an entryway. It read, *Thor's Hammer*.

"We're going to a pub?"

"Sure. Why not?"

Morgan shot him a brilliant smile.

When he saw her face light up, he wanted to kiss her right there and then. Instead, he thrust the thought out of his head and waited for her to pull off her helmet as he had, so he could lead her inside. "Skord owns this place and dozens more like it across Europe."

"I feel something. It's like a kind of energy running through me."

"Vampires. There are many who frequent this place." He nodded toward some men and women exiting the pub. "But you should be feeling more positive sensations than what you felt with the rogues."

She nodded in agreement. "Yeah. It's not like rogues at all. This energy seems…*pure*. But why don't I feel this around you?"

"You probably did at first, but you were newly changed so the sensation would have been very weak. Your need for blood blocked anything else out. You're used to me now. It's sort of like getting into a tub of hot water and feeling the heat at first, then getting used to it as you sit there. You understand?"

"I guess so," she answered as she scratched the side of her neck. "That tingling is getting worse."

Sean saw her discomfort and tried to explain. "Some of

the men and women in here are very powerful. Older than both of us put together. But they're safe. They're what we refer to as *independents*. They don't owe their allegiance to anyone, but they aren't evil like the rogues. The blood they're drinking is purchased through ordinary blood donation companies. Most of it is unfit for human consumption. Humans can't use blood if it's been refrigerated at temperatures too cold, too warm, or if the expiration date goes by. Instead of letting it go to waste, Skord and other independents buy it posing as representatives from medical labs and companies specializing in the destruction of biohazards. What isn't suitable for humans is more than good enough for us." After entering and finding a table away from the entrance, he pulled out a chair for her. "Here, sit down and I'll get us something to drink."

They put their helmets on their chosen table but left their coats on to hide the weapons they carried.

Sean stepped a few yards away. He spoke to a pretty

waitress for a few moments and returned with two pewter mugs full of fresh blood. He sat one in front of her and took his own seat beside her.

"I assume none of the humans knows what we're drinking?" she asked.

"No. When you go into a bar owned by a vampire, which, let's face it, would be the only bar you could ever drink in…you order yourself a *Lunar Stout.* You're automatically telling the vampire waiter or waitress to bring you blood in some kind of container that hides what you're drinking. And those humans around you don't hear you use the word blood."

Morgan stared.

"What's wrong?"

"You people have this all worked out, don't you? Even down to how you order a drink in public."

"Our kind, which now includes *you,* had a few thousand years to figure all this out."

Morgan picked up the mug and sipped the blood. "Uh, Sean?"

"Yes?"

"Why does this taste different from what we have at Greenwood?"

"It's Skord's own brew. He puts a couple of teaspoons of his own blood into the vat."

Morgan choked and put the mug down as if it were red-hot. "That's not funny."

Sean raised one brow. "I wasn't trying to be." He looked over her head. "And you can ask Skord yourself."

***

The hair on the back of her neck stood up when Sean got out of his chair and walked around the table. Morgan slowly stood and turned. She kept looking up but wasn't sure if she'd ever see the part of the pub owner where his head should be situated. As tall as Sean was, this man dwarfed every human being Morgan had ever met. He stood nearly seven feet tall and looked as if he could kill a person just by backhanding them.

"Morgan, I want you to meet Skord Shorner. He's the best friend I've ever had."

Skord bowed slightly and held out his hand.

Morgan took it and smiled up at the handsome, chivalrous giant before resuming her seat at the table with them.

"Sean has told me about you and I was hoping we could meet," Skord announced. "He and I have known each other many years. I hope you'll consider me a friend." He patted Sean on the shoulder and clasped hands firmly with his Irish comrade.

Morgan noted Skord's thick German accent, his fascinating face and his long tawny hair. It was currently pulled back at the nape of his neck.

As handsome as Sean was, Skord was equally blessed. He had a kind twinkle in his blue eyes that chased away her initial fear. And though she sensed great strength about him, she inherently sensed goodness too. All-in-all, she trusted Sean's appraisal of the man and continued to study Skord's strong jaw and hair as he spoke. The muscular build under the big man's sweater turned female heads though Skord didn't seem to notice.

Skord leaned forward and spoke concisely. "I heard about your problem with the rogues, Morgan. Sean asked me to find out what I could. Unfortunately, I haven't been able to learn much," he admitted. "But I'll keep trying."

"Thanks," Sean told him, then got to the meat of his visit. "I wanted to talk to you about the offer you made in reference to helping Morgan…if she needed to get started again."

Morgan stared at both of them for a moment, but she directed her question to Skord. "I take it that if I don't want in the agency, I'll need to contact you? Is that it?"

Skord nodded. "I was with *The Nightwatchers* at one

time and still make a routine call to them every month as procedure requires. Fergus MacArtan, the head of the agency, trusts me."

Morgan fell silent for a moment, thinking about what had just been said.

Sean momentarily stared at the tabletop and voiced his opinion. "I honestly believe that if it were totally up to Fergus *personally*, he'd probably let you go anywhere you wanted, Morgan. But he's one of the council members as well as the organization's leaders. As such, he has promised to uphold a list of rules and regulations established for our mutual safety. Fergus would have no other choice in the matter but to make sure you aren't a threat. Skord might be better equipped to keep you safe in that event."

"I'm not fooled." She looked at both the men before continuing. "If they'd kill my uncle for not recruiting me the right way, they'd do the same to me. And this is a way of getting me to safety before the agency can find out what happened."

Skord leaned back and sipped some of the blood from his mug. "Forgive me for considering your beauty first instead of your intelligence. It's a stupid thing men do sometimes."

Morgan shot him a half-smile, then glared angrily at Sean. "When were you going to tell me you set up this safety-net involving Skord? And who was supposed to do the deed if I proved to be too much trouble?"

Sean's gaze fell.

"*You* were going to kill me?" she quietly asked as she stared at Sean.

Skord responded for his friend. "He wouldn't have done it, Morgan. I'm certain I could have intervened on your behalf with Fergus."

Though she spoke to the bigger man, she kept a steady gaze on Sean. "You'd have *tried,* Skord. I only just met you and you'd have truly tried." She looked down at the rough-hewn, wooden tabletop for a long moment. "Sean would have followed his orders. If they'd told him to kill me, he would have. I was fooling myself into believing otherwise, though I knew he'd be the one to take me out all along." She addressed Sean with her next comment. "Your job means more to you than anything, doesn't it? You'd have actually taken my head off, wouldn't you? Just admit it."

Sean put his mug down, angrily slid it across the table, and glared at her. "What do you want me to say? I've brought you to a friend. We'd already planned how to keep you safe and would have risked both our own hides doing it?"

Skord leaned toward Morgan and said, "It won't come to that. I won't let it."

Morgan considered Skord's resolve and had to ask the big man some obvious questions. "Why? Why would you risk your life for a complete stranger when Sean, the man who changed me, wouldn't risk *his*?"

Skord took her hand in his. "You and I aren't strangers any longer. We know each other *now*. And any man who could take one look at you and contemplate such a thing doesn't deserve to exist," he declared. "Sean wouldn't have hurt you and neither will I."

Morgan picked up her drink and remained silent.

***

Sean sat there seething over her mistrust of *him;* after all *he'd* done for her. She was certain he'd take her life when he'd just proven how far he'd go to keep her safe. He sensed a deep, painful anger inside Morgan. It was a mixture of harsh emotions he hadn't sensed from her before. Certainly not to this degree and not so much he could conclude she'd finally had enough…enough of *what* was the issue. He couldn't understand her attitude and its resulting antagonism being directed at him when all he'd done was try to help. Surely, she knew in her heart he'd have never been the one to destroy her, no matter what his orders commanded. "I…I think we'd better go," Sean tactfully told Skord. He waited for Morgan to stand up, but she simply sat there staring at him as if she didn't know him any longer. He knew he'd need to persuade her that she'd always be safe in his presence, but fate stepped in and his argument was never aired. A waitress appeared beside Skord. The girl handed her boss a note and then walked away.

Skord quickly read the missive, looked at Sean and said, "Don't go."

"What's wrong?" Sean asked.

"Rogues. They've evidently been watching Greenwood from a distance so you couldn't sense their presence. They knew when you and Morgan left tonight and sent word ahead, to the rest of their ilk. Some of them are just outside in the alley, wanting to send a message."

Sean finished off the last of his blood, sat the mug back on the table, and picked up his helmet. "I'll get them out of Dublin, keep Morgan here."

"Like hell!" she countered while keeping her voice low and retrieving her own headgear.

"You don't understand," Skord softly advised. "They don't want Morgan. They want *you*, Sean. They want to talk…they say Regar is with them and he wants to see you." He handed the note to Sean and waited.

Sean took it, read the message, and then glanced around before speaking again. "Do you believe they're telling the truth, Skord?"

"Who's Regar?" Morgan asked.

Sean quickly shot back an answer. "Someone you don't need to know about."

"Yes, she does," Skord reasoned. "She's one of us now."

"If somebody doesn't tell me what the hell is going on, I'm walking," Morgan angrily threatened.

"You should have told her," Skord insisted. "It's not right that she doesn't know."

Sean pushed his hair back with one hand, turned to Morgan, and leaned very near her so no one could hear.

"Listen carefully because I'm going to say this *very* fast and only once."

She simply nodded.

"Regar is a very crafty vampire. He has a healthy dislike of humans and vampires intermingling. He doesn't like *The Nightwatchers*, never has, and would do anything to disrupt operations or put a stop to them altogether. He's gotten in the middle of our business before, and we're pretty sure he's had his hand in all kinds of crap from illegal arms sales to buying and selling women. He's as elusive as hell. No one in this century has ever seen his face that we know of. The man has probably had as many names and identities as there are stars in the sky, but *we've* always referred to him as *Regar*." Sean continued at an even faster rate. "He sends his minions to do his work and it's rumored even *they* don't know what he really looks like. He's an ancient who might be thousands of years old and that makes him very powerful. And, as if being a very powerful vampire wasn't enough, we believe he can probably get his hands on untold fortunes. So…what he can't do himself, he can certainly pay others to accomplish on his behalf. Now…any more questions, *Morgan*?"

"No…I think that about covers it."

Sean didn't miss her pretended meek response.

"The note says Sean is to meet Regar at midnight, at an old stone circle; the closest one to Greenwood," Skord uttered then added, "I'm coming along."

"Why?" Morgan asked. "You know this is probably a setup. Especially if rogues are involved and especially since they attacked us on the moors."

Sean had to agree on that point. "Yes, but if there's one chance in a million we could actually meet Regar in person, and finally put a modern face to the name, then we have to take it."

Morgan sat back in her chair and glared at them both. "And what am I supposed to do? Put a candle in the window and wait?"

"Your sarcasm doesn't cut it with me, Morgan. Skord and I will take you back to the compound and drop you off at the door. Tell Danielle what happened. She'll know what to do if I don't come back." He saw her open her mouth to argue. "That's an order, Morgan! This isn't Los Angeles. You're not ready for this kind of confrontation. Skord has backed me up before. We went through WWII together and we know each other's moves."

***

Morgan lagged behind as Sean and Skord got up and headed for the rear entrance. Silently fuming over the curt dismissal, she angrily tossed her helmet up and down and followed the two men. Something in Skord's eyes and the tone of his voice, convinced Morgan that her new German friend was telling the total truth about trying to help her. But Sean hadn't even let her in on their mutual plan to get her away safely. He couldn't even trust her enough to tell her there *would* be a way out through Skord. And all this time she assumed she'd just have to get the best survival training she could while pretending to join the agency. Then, one day while the agency's guard was down, she'd probably have made a run for it. That was the way the scenario had played itself out in her mind. And she'd have left everything and everyone in this new life behind, including her uncle and Dani. They'd be heartbroken she had run, but they'd be glad she was alive and might even covertly help. In many ways, it would be like dying all over again. Sean, in his infinite wisdom, hadn't even allowed her to agree or disagree with his and Skord's escape plans on her behalf and she knew why.

Fear he felt from past events kept him from treating her like an equal, and he'd always be trying to save her from something whether the risk was real or only perceived. Now, he was about to face some enemy old and powerful enough to put the fear of God into him and his best friend, and she wasn't allowed to even help. And unlike the previous encounter with the rogues, she *knew* she could stand with

Sean and Skord, as a team. *"Son-of-a-bitch!"* she quietly groused when she joined the men at the back of the pub.

"I heard that," Sean replied, then carefully cracked open the back door.

Skord's guard approached, nodded, and pointed to the empty alley.

"They've gone," Skord advised. "Let me get my bike and I'll follow you to Greenwood, Sean."

***

Sean didn't trust himself to say another word to Morgan. Defiantly, she seemed quite happy to wallow in martyred anger. The situation was such that he should want to get her out of his life as soon as possible, but he perversely found himself physically responding to her flashing green eyes and show of fine Irish temper. There was something about her silent fury that just flat turned him on, though it was the most inappropriate time to have those emotions. Nevertheless, they were there. His body was hard with need.

He silently waited for Skord to return. The big man showed up a few moments later; all in black leather. His helmet was equally dark colored. The clothing almost forecast the fight to come.

"My bike is parked near yours, Sean. I think it'll be safe to leave now. Rogues are ignorant but they aren't going to try something on a main street in the middle of Dublin."

Sean faced Morgan, then draped his arm around her body. "You hang on tight in case we have to drive fast." He didn't miss the *go-to-hell* look she shot him.

He made sure she was securely on his bike, waited for Skord to position himself directly behind them, and then took off after all helmets were in place.

The trip back to Greenwood was made in total silence. Sean drove into the compound through the main gate while Skord waited on the road outside the compound. Once he was at the front door, Sean shut off his bike and physically led Morgan to the foyer.

"I want you to stay put. You don't go outside this house until I get back," he ordered. "Do you understand?"

"Yeah. I hear you," she told him as they simultaneously pulled their helmets off. But why didn't Skord come in with us?"

"Since he isn't with the agency, he's technically prohibited from entering the compound. He'll wait for me. He knows I've got to get to the armory and find a weapon more appropriate than the one I'm carrying," Sean conveyed. "It might not be a bad idea to keep that crossbow of yours handy, though I don't think even Regar has the balls to order his people into the compound," Sean informed her as he tried to alleviate any fear. "If anything *should* happen, get Dani and the staff to the basement, lock it off and stay there. Is that clear?"

She nodded.

"When the sun rises, the human guards will summon help. That's our procedure. You follow it," Sean firmly told her, then left Morgan and raced toward the armory.

***

If you plan to continue with the series, there is another chapter…but I suggest you stop here if you don't like cliffhangers leading to the next book in The Nightwatchers saga.

Thanks for reading!

Chapter 7

Morgan went in search of Dani, but couldn't resist mumbling, "If you think I'm gonna sit here like a sack of potatoes, you're full of shit, Sean Reilly!"

The next time Morgan saw Sean, he was coming up from the basement and still wore his black leather duster, presumably to cover the long sword he carried beneath it. The obligatory helmet was gripped in his right hand.

Before he went out the door, Sean turned to both the women. "You know what to do, Dani. I've given Morgan instructions which I'm *sure* she'll obey."

Morgan walked toward him. "This isn't right. You should be taking a lot more people with you. There were five rogues on the moors the night I ran. They'll bring more tonight," she warned. "I can pretty well guess they don't want to *talk* and you damned well know it. Otherwise, you wouldn't be making these backup plans."

"Yes, there were five rogues, and we took them out with nothing more than our bare hands. Or, in your case, a kick to the groin," he swiftly admitted. "But I have to do this my way."

"All this just to catch a glimpse of this Regar character? Is this clown really worth it?"

"If you knew how much trouble he has caused, you wouldn't ask that question. Not that I need to justify myself, but if Fergus MacArtan were here, he'd give me full permission to act as I deem appropriate."

Sean turned to go, but swiftly turned back.

Morgan stood stiffly as he wrapped his hand around the back of her neck, pulled her forward, and kissed her hard. "For luck," he told her.

Morgan watched him leave, waited until the sound of his engine faded into the distance, and then quickly turned her attention to Danielle. "Where's the nearest stone circle? That's where this is all going down."

"Morgan, you can't seriously—"

"If you don't tell me, I'll look it up on a computer in the library. We've got less than two hours for me to find them and catch up. That's if the rogues haven't lied about an ambush and really *will* wait until midnight. I wouldn't count on that, Dani. Sean doesn't trust them. That's why he and Skord are leaving now and not waiting. I'm in the position of having to run cross-country so the sound of a car engine won't alert anyone I'm coming."

"He's given you orders to stay."

"I'm not one of his people. He can't order me to do anything."

Dani passed a shaking hand over her face. "He'll be furious."

"*Dani*?"

Dani relented. "Oh, what the bloody hell! You *will* go, won't you? Even if I call in the guards?"

"The guards are human. Though I'm sure they're very

well trained, they wouldn't have a chance against my greater strength and speed. One of them might even get hurt and I'd hate to do that."

Dani sighed heavily. "All right, Morgan. But first you need to get to the armory and choose some weapons. Afterward, I'll map out a route to the stone circle. If you run hard, you can get there soon enough. As you've said, we can assume Sean and Skord intend to get there first and lay out a plan in case this is a trap, or they'd have done the same thing you're about to do."

"Might work better this way," Morgan murmured, "Nobody will know I'm coming and I'll be damned quiet."

For the next twenty minutes, Morgan gathered the things she needed and perused a map Dani gave her. She reckoned she could be at the stone circle maybe half an hour after Skord and Sean, if she ran fast and used the speed she knew she had. What happened afterward was up to the rogues. There still wasn't one instinct in her that didn't scream *ambush.*

When she was ready to leave, Morgan sketched out her preferred cross-country route on a piece of paper and gave it to Dani. "This is the way I'm going. There are hiding places I've marked in case I need to outrun the sun. Give me five minutes to get to the outside wall, then turn off the perimeter alarm. Fifteen seconds more to let me get over the wall and clear, then turn the alarm back on. My leaving won't be detected. Got it?"

"Oh, Morgan! Patrick would have my head for letting you do this. Never mind what Sean will do."

"My uncle knows me better than anyone. I'm only sorry Sean never got to know me at all though I guess that's a discussion for another time. I'm outta here."

Morgan pulled on black leather gloves and never looked back. She headed for the outside wall and knew Danielle would turn off the alarm just as requested. She looked at her watch, judged it was time, and lept over the fence as if the motion were only child's play. Then she moved away once her feet touched ground on the other side. "Somebody's really got to upgrade the alarm. This is too easy," she quietly confirmed.

She ran toward the northwestern night sky, as fast as she could. And never, in her entire life, had she felt such a sense of purpose or strength. It was like being a cop again—only the stakes were much higher. She silently prayed she could get to Sean and Skord before something horrible happened.

According to what Sean told her, Regar was as evil as an entity could get, and had all the power necessary to take out whoever got in his way. It was logical to assume a vampire so potent would know his message would be taken *quite* seriously. Sean would be obligated to respond to it; to find out what was going on. Regar, for whatever reason, had used this particular time in history to lure both Sean *and* Skord out in the open. Regar had known the two of them were at the pub; it followed that he understood Skord would go with his best friend. Of course, the meeting might be legitimate. Regar might actually want to just *talk*.

Morgan's instincts told her otherwise. She didn't want to see Sean die for having taken the chance that duty required. They hadn't had time to call in vampiric backup from the organization and a human guard, untrained with meeting a bunch of rogues, would certainly die. Morgan assumed that's why none of the guards had been taken even though they'd have probably volunteered if they'd known. While she hadn't been on more than speaking terms with any of the staff, including the guards, they all seemed to greatly respect Sean and did whatever he asked, without question. That was the mark of a good leader. But who would lead them next if something happened to him?

Morgan dug into herself and moved even faster. A fine drizzle began making the slopes and hills treacherous. But she kept running.

***

Sean stood on the hillside and looked up at the stone circle. "I think this is as close as we get for now."

"I don't sense anything," Skord said as he perused their surroundings. His sword hilt was clasped firmly in one hand but was sheathed as yet.

"Neither do I. We both know someone as old as Regar could easily hide his people. He'd have tricks up his sleeve that no one has ever heard of."

Skord nodded in agreement. "I hear he came from Gaul originally."

"I know others have seen him in a different century, but he surely wouldn't look the same now. Regar's probably a man of a thousand faces." The night breeze picked up as the drizzle fell. Sean had to push his hair out of his eyes and shake strands of it back over his shoulder.

"Why the hell don't you tie your hair back like mine? It's going to get in your way," Skord complained while he kept the better part of his attention on the surrounding hills.

"Just call it a desire to be attuned to my ancient Celtic heritage," Sean quipped. "I like it loose."

"Sure. It'll look grand, flying in the breeze as some rogue puts your head on a pike someday!"

"You first," Sean smilingly shot back. "And why the shaggin' hell are you even posing such an inane question right now?"

Skord shot him a lop-sided grin. "Ever since the Sixties, you've worn it the same damn way. It's one of those questions I always wanted to ask, and I might not get the chance later."

When an icy sensation crept up his spine, Sean grasped the hilt of his sword and drew it. He heard Skord do the same. "Well then, it's shaggin' good you *did* ask…we've got company."

"Shall we meet them where we are, or make our way into the circle?"

"By St. Patrick's cap, if I'm going to be outnumbered,

let's get this over with in the middle of a sacred place. No better location for warriors to meet."

"Since Germans historically considered these circles as sacred as the Irish, I agree," Skord answered and moved forward at Sean's right side.

Only five minutes later, Sean and Skord stood in the middle of the old stone circle, back to back. They'd been together on so many assignments that Sean knew Skord would gauge every move and counter with a defensive one of his own. "Come on out you rotting sons-of-bitches!" Sean dared.

He watched as four rogues entered the circle in front of him, as if they'd moved from the mists of the landscape. Silently, they came forward with blades raised. He sensed there were at least as many facing Skord. But there were others in the hillsides. Their putrid emanation was everywhere. The man he took to be their leader, a tall particularly emaciated rogue, approached while brandishing a wicked-looking Italian sword. Sean braced himself for whatever might happen.

"I'm called Berrigan," the rogue leader said as he tossed an object at Sean, then reached in his hip pocket to toss several more like it around the stone circle.

Sean easily caught the disc thrown at him with his free hand; his sword still brandished in the other. He looked down at the object now lying in his palm. It was a talisman—an old coin, coated in blood-red enamel with a large R in the center. Even without his preternatural site, the moon's glow shone down on the coin leaving no doubt about its owner. "I assume this is Regar's calling card. I'm wondering why the likes of him would need to recruit you bunch of *scum*?"

"We aren't with him!" Berrigan announced. "But when agents from *The Nightwatchers* find these coins at the place where you two died, your people and Regar's will be at open war with one another. We'll be able to move about freely as neither side will have time to hunt us down."

"Don't shit me on this because I know you're aware of it...why did your kind go after the woman from the compound?" Sean loudly demanded. "Or is it you never wanted her to begin with, but were lying in wait for *me*?" Sean kept his hand tightly wrapped around the sword hilt as he spoke, but simultaneously tucked the coin he'd caught in a hip pocket. He expected a sudden attack and squared his body for it.

Berrigan slowly approached Sean's position. "She was fresh meat. Ready and available. Nothing more. Her presence outside your walls was a happy coincidence for a pack of my people who were hunting nearby. The scent of her was...*most* alluring."

"And why is it you want *Sean*?" Skord asked, while keeping his eyes on those rogues in front of him.

Berrigan paused. "I am not obligated to explain. But if knowing the answer will enrage you and make our vengeance sweeter, then I will respond."

Sean groaned and uttered, "*Sweet Jesus* here it comes…the obligatory *explain-to-the-victim* speech. It *always* comes right before the heroes are attacked." He shook his head. "You know, Skord, rogues can be so stupidly *predictable.*"

Skord laugh at the insult.

Berrigan snarled in anger, then moved closer and stopped just a few feet in front of Sean. "Do you remember your mission in Prague some months ago?"

"Prague?" Sean repeated, "I don't know that I've ever been there."

"I hear it's beautiful this time of year," Skord poetically supplied.

"To joke at our expense isn't wise!" Berrigan furiously warned.

Sean grinned. "If you mean to kill us, what's the difference? Now get to your point."

Berrigan scowled. "You were on a mission when my

brother was killed, *Nightwatcher*. It was by your hand he died…I want your head!"

Sean raised his sword higher and knew without a doubt that Skord had done the same. They were very firmly back-to-back now. "Oh, yes…*that* trip to Prague. Seems there were some foolish rogues who got mixed up in selling a biological weapon on the illegal market; some new kind of spore that could wipe out grain crops worldwide if I recall."

Skord nudged him from behind. "You just relayed classified information. Fergus MacArtan will be outraged!" he joked.

"Something tells me our friend Berrigan already knows about that mission. If Fergus wants a piece of my ass, he'll have to stand in line," Sean quipped.

Berrigan pointed one boney finger at Sean. "It was our business! You and your people have interfered with my kind for the last time."

Sean shook his head at the dereliction of logic. "I guess

you didn't give a damn about who your brother was selling the shit to. Or what someone would use it for?"

"We have a right to survive," Berrigan argued.

"And how long do you think you'd do so without humans, you *idiot*!" Skord blurted. "Kill humans and *all* vampires die!"

Sean waited a full thirty seconds while Berrigan glanced at the ground from left to right as if he had no answer to that insightful truth. Finally, the brainless rogue—rendered more obtuse by the too-frequent consumption of vampire flesh—visibly shook in anger and glared at *him*.

Berrigan shouted his next comment. "You set yourself up as judge, juror, and executioner. All with the approval of dozens of countries whose own people don't know you kill at will."

"And your brother wasn't going to hurt anyone with those spores, was he?" Sean sarcastically reiterated.

Skord let out a frustrated sigh before saying, "This

sounds like one of those *I'll rule the world* scenarios."

"They've been watching too many old spy flicks," Sean jested.

"While eating vampire finger food and drinking blood chasers," Skord shot back.

Berrigan growled in fury. "*Enough*! You and the German will die. Regar will get the blame and we'll get on with our business. And just to make the victory complete, I'll have the new meat you have stored at your compound, *Nightwatcher*. She'll be quite a treat after we frighten her enough to tenderize her flesh."

Sean had no time to remark. The first swing was Berrigan's, but *he* parried it and sliced the rogue's slender left hand off.

The other rogues rushed in.

He wasn't sorry for having brought Skord along. His friend had no direct quarrel with the rogues, but he knew there wasn't any place Skord would rather be.

While fending off a downward blow from a cutlass, Sean felt a dagger go deep into his side. It was delivered by one of the hidden rogues who ran into the circle. That man lost his head by the edge of *his* blade and wouldn't be fighting again.

Still, others came.

He fought like a Celtic warrior of old. And just like his ancestors, the battle lust was on him. He struck out with blinding speed even though his wound was barely healing. He heard Skord beating back some of those rogues to the rear, and still more came.

For the first time since WWII, Sean feared for his life. There was a time after that war was over that he wanted to die, but not *now*. And he wondered if half the rogue world had shown up just to see him and his German friend fall. It seemed they kept bolting forward from the surrounding hills; more and more appeared with lightning speed.

***

From some distance left of the stone circle, Morgan looked at the scene with complete revulsion. The fighting she saw was like something out of a medieval movie. Two men in black leather were back-to-back, standing off no less than fifteen rogues. As one would move forward and slash at Sean or Skord, another would run in and lunge, keeping both the defenders from ably protecting themselves. "Why the hell didn't they just ignore that stupid note," she groused. "*Men*! They think with their fucking testicles!"

She silently ran forward, keeping her guard up for any strange sensations, just the way Sean had taught her.

When she got to within a few hundred feet of the fighting, one rogue jumped from behind a large rock and pointed a wicked looking saber at her. She swung once, cut him right across the throat, and watched him fall. He struggled to stem the flow of blood, but she knew he wouldn't rise again. His head lolled sideways and fell.

"That's for pointing that nasty thing at me!" she yelled,

as she ran past him.

Then she ran into the circle from one side, fighting for all she was worth. But the fight didn't seem to last much longer. She saw Sean's sword swiftly pierce the body of one taller rogue who moved in too soon, ahead of his compatriots. Then with a determined swing, Sean took the rogue's head.

Her own fight began with another rather vicious looking attacker saw her. She had no time to witness anything else.

She fought as she'd been trained and felt the absolute rush of pure adrenaline, or something very much like it, enter her veins. Her strength and speed seemed to grow with each parry and thrust. She felt her incisors extend to a dangerously sharp length. She heard a noise very much like a big panther roaring and was surprised the sound came from her own throat. Her sword arm worked until every rogue in front of her was down. Too late, she heard Skord's shout of warning.

"Morgan…behind you!"

She turned just in time to see one last rogue rushing in and was set to battle him properly, but Sean ran in front of her with speed she couldn't imagine. He took the downward slash of a long sword in her stead and neatly killed the man who'd swung at her. Then her rescuer fell to his knees with his hands protecting the lower part of his abdomen.

"That's the last of them," Skord claimed as he rushed forward to help his friend.

With the lust to fight spent, Morgan knelt beside Sean and put one hand on his cheek. "Let me see." She pulled at his hands until he released his grip on the lower portion of his body. "*Oh my God!* He's almost been eviscerated." She gazed up at Skord. "What do we do?"

"You don't bloody well do anything, you little banshee! I told you to stay at Greenwood!" Sean ranted as he clumsily stood, re-sheathed his sword, and then fell to the ground again.

"Argue about it later," Skord muttered. "We need to

get you back to the compound. All the rogues we fought are either dead, or they won't heal in time to get out of the sun. They're in no shape to even dig into the ground, but that doesn't mean more aren't on their way!"

Morgan vehemently nodded in agreement.

Skord re-sheathed his sword, grabbed Sean, and hefted him over his shoulder. "I'll get him back to his motorcycle. If you ride with him, it'll be safer than trying to run cross-country. As we move down the hill, keep an eye on our backs. If any of those vermin in the hills get near, take their heads."

She was on the verge of running to those rogues still left alive and taking them out if for no other reason than to end their suffering. Sean had told her if the sun came up on a vampire, wounded or not, that was that. Their carcasses and residual blood- spill would fry up; no trace would be left. But there simply wasn't time to tend to the task. Instinct warned her other rogues were approaching.

She kept her attention riveted on the area of the circle,

as Skord and Sean moved down the embankment and toward the two motorcycles. As the big German had commanded, she backed her way down the hill, protecting their retreat. Her sword was aimed high while scanning the hills. Nothing came forward...*yet*.

They quickly made it to the cycles. That was when howls echoed in the hillsides. From their vantage point in the rocky areas, rogues could have easily seen their fallen comrades.

"*Jesus*...we need to move!" she warned and then watched as Skord carefully maneuvered Sean onto the back of his own motorcycle.

"You'll have to hang onto Morgan," Skord advised, "there isn't room on my bike for you *and* me."

Morgan noted Sean's silence even as the big German quickly turned to her with a pleading expression on his face.

"*Please* tell me you can you drive a damn motorcycle," Skord begged.

"Watch me," she asserted.

As Skord mounted his bike, she re-sheathed her weapon, and hopped on the seat in front of Sean. She felt one arm go tightly about her body, but the other was virtually holding his intestines in place.

She knew why he wasn't healing any better than the injured rogues at the stone circle. If a wound inflicted by a silver blade went too deep, healing would take time. That was what Sean had taught her, and the proof was in the injury done to his body. "Morgan…you're *not* driving my bike," Sean brokenly complained then groaned in obvious agony.

"Shut up!" Morgan shouted, then grabbed his helmet off the ground where he'd left it and jammed it on his head. "Wear this. It's the frickin' law!"

"We'd better hurry, Morgan. He needs to lie down," Skord warned.

Morgan did as Skord suggested, started the motorcycle, and headed down the road leading back to Greenwood. It took some time for her to maneuver the winding curves and narrow lanes while trying to keep Sean from falling off. She had to repeatedly put one hand behind her to find his waist and steady him. The farther they went, the more concerned for him she became.

Just as she heard him gasp in pain, they rounded a curve and Greenwood lay ahead of them. She drove up to the front gates with speed. And though the wrought iron gates swung open automatically, she saw several guards rush forward. They let her in but were simultaneously insisting Skord must stay outside.

"Let him in the damn compound," Sean rasped, "I-I'll take responsibility."

The guards nodded and waved Skord through the gate, closing it behind them.

Just as Morgan pulled up to the front doors, Dani opened them and trotted forward. The older woman seemed oblivious to the fact that Skord was inside the perimeter.

Morgan assumed Dani had been alerted by the gate guards and knew Skord's help would be needed to get a man Sean's size up to his room. The guards behind them were too busy for the task. All of them were now rushing to the walls to make sure the attack on their boss wasn't about to spread into the compound.

All Morgan could do was watch as a flourish of activity took place.

In lightning speed, she saw Skord pull his and Sean's helmets off. The larger man then hoisted Sean into his arms. They moved inside the building while Dani shouted orders to the household staff. They, in turn, ran to do as she commanded.

For Morgan, it was like watching a very action-packed movie scene. She finally pulled her head together, ran forward, and caught up with Dani and the others as they climbed the stairs toward Sean's room.

Used to the turmoil that could take place at the scene of

police shootings, she *wasn't* at all experienced with the aftermath of vampire attacks. Only years of law enforcement experience kept her acting rationally. Sean's tutoring notwithstanding, this had been one hell of a night.

"He'll be all right, won't he?" Morgan quickly asked as she caught up with the group headed to Sean's room.

It was Dani who responded.

"I'm not sure, Morgan. Wounds like the one rogues deliver are very dangerous. Or so I'm told."

"But he's going to be okay, right?"

Dani paused in the hallway and simply stared at her for a very long moment. She suddenly murmured something about making sure enough blood was available and rushed away. Morgan was left to figure out what to do next.

She chose to bolt after Skord and Sean. The door to Sean's room was open when she got there, so she didn't bother knocking or announcing herself. Skord had already lowered Sean's body to his bed. From where she stood, Sean's wound looked even more gruesome than it did on the moors. Blood flowed freely from the open gash and internal matter oozed forth.

She stood motionless as Skord found a towel from the bathroom and tried to wipe away most of the loose gore. He soon tossed his towel-blotter to one side and began to undress Sean.

Morgan felt she should have left, but she simply couldn't. Instead, she moved forward and removed the tall leather boots Sean wore, then searched for any supply of ready blood she could find.

A small refrigerator yielded two full bottles. She turned around and held them out to Skord, just as he pulled a blanket over Sean's nude body. There was only a glimpse of steely muscle but it was enough to dry her mouth. Presumably, the covering was for modesty's sake. She didn't ask but assumed Skord wouldn't want Dani running in and seeing Sean lying there with his guts hanging loose. The big, sweet German got points for tact. But when Skord finally took one of the bottles of blood from her, she saw his face and knew something was wrong. His next words confirmed this instinct.

"I don't think this blood is going to do," Skord pointedly announced.

"Why? It's supposed to be fresh. Isn't that what Sean needs?"

"He needs blood that's *more potent.*"

Morgan got the distinct feeling there was some tidbit of information she hadn't been told; some small piece of news that Sean had held back, or he'd meant to impart and had never found the time or inclination to explain. Before she could question the big German about it, Dani walked in with several more bottles of blood. As the bad scene took a turn for the worse, Morgan heard Sean moan again.

"Get Morgan out of here," he insisted, "she doesn't need to be involved with this."

Skord ignored the order, opened the blood bottle he'd

just taken from Morgan and put it to Sean's lips.

Morgan saw her injured trainer wince in pain as the swallowed blood settled in his torn gut. She put down the rest of her blood reserve and waited to see what happened, but nothing on Sean's body healed.

"What kind of silver could make a vampire keep bleeding like that?" Morgan softly asked and felt an overwhelming compulsion to go to Sean and hold him.

"Don't worry, dear," Dani comforted. "The silver causing the cut was likely very pure, but he won't die. His heart wasn't pierced. It's just the blood we have isn't fresh enough to seal a very bad wound…at least not soon. He needs something…*stronger.*"

Skord nodded then re-examined the wound. "Looks like someone *did* swing a pure, silver blade right into you, Sean. The metal was too soft to fight a lengthy battle, but *sterling* enough to damage one of us. Wonder where the bastards got a hold of a blade- master to craft such a weapon?"

Sean pulled the bedspread higher and pressed it into his abdomen to help staunch the ooze.

Skord turned to Dani and explained what had happened out on the moors, but Morgan ignored the rehashing of the story. She wasn't concerned with the past; only what they were supposed to do about a nasty, gaping wound. She chewed on her lower lip while watching Sean grow paler.

"So what do we do people?" she loudly queried. "Sean is still bleeding, you know!"

When Dani and Skord stared at her, Morgan felt one of those *what the crap is going on* sensations. Before she could ask anything else, Skord spoke.

"Sean needs *cold* blood. No matter how fresh human blood is it won't work as well."

"Okay…what the hell is *cold* blood?"

Appearing to ignore her question entirely, Skord and Dani walked into the hall as if some kind of confab were in the works.

"Oh…great…just walk away," Morgan criticized as she threw her hands in the air in absolute frustration.

From his bed, Sean attempted an explanation. "The wound will heal, Morgan. It's just…when a vampire is hurt very badly, human blood doesn't help us mend quickly. I need amplified blood."

"I still don't know what that—"

"Not to digress, but guess how much trouble you're in, you little pain-in-the-neck!" he warned. "What in the name of all the Irish saints did you think you were doing out there? You could have been butchered."

"First, that's not answering my question," she shot back. "Second, I might very well have just saved your vampiric butt!"

"I ought to lock you in your room and throw the shaggin' key away! Why didn't you do as I ordered?" Sean bitched.

Morgan glowered at him. "You're welcome…for saving your life."

Sean pointed toward his abdomen. "I got this wound defending you."

"If you hadn't jumped in the frickin' way, I'd have handled that rogue and you'd still be hauling your damn bowels inside…*where they belong*."

She was about to continue her argument when Danielle appeared at the door, called out her name and motioned her into the hall.

"Go on, Morgan. See what Dani wants," he tersely commanded.

Morgan got up to leave, but he grabbed her hand to hold her there for a moment longer.

"Don't think this conversation is over. You got out of the compound with help and I can guess who your accomplice was. This is what I get for not chaining you to a wall. Next time, I'll know better."

There wouldn't be a next time. Morgan had already made up her mind about that, and about something else as well.

Dani called out to her again and interrupted her train of thought. Sean motioned for her to go, so she left him and walked into the hallway. Skord and Dani were standing there waiting for her. From the looks on their faces, she knew a monumental *factoid* was on the way; something she might not like. They glanced at each other as though one was waiting for the other to speak first.

Dani put a hand on Morgan's shoulder. "Morgan, dear, Sean needs fresher blood or he's going to linger with that wound for days."

"He said it would heal."

Dani shook her head in denial. "The wound is bad. It was inflicted by a rogue who knew exactly what he was doing. The way Skord tells it, the rogues were probably trying to get in that one cut all along and take his head later. They wanted to see him suffer." She took a deep breath before continuing. "Sean *will* heal all right, but he'll be in pain for days, as I've said. If, however, he gets fresher blood…he'll be right as rain in no time."

Morgan looked at the giant of a man who was staring at the toes of his boots. There was some facet of this conversation that clearly made the big man uncomfortable. "Can't we get fresher blood from some of the guards?"

Dani stared at Skord.

Skord cleared his throat and waved a hand toward Sean's room. "Uh, I'll be helping Sean. This is something that would be better coming from you, Dani. Someone should have told Morgan about this."

Morgan watched Skord walk away, then she turned her attention back to the other woman. "Why do I get the idea I've just been drafted into something?"

Dani smirked. "It isn't as bad as you think. In fact, you might rather enjoy the experience. Or so I'm told."

***

For the next fifteen minutes, Morgan listened to what Dani told her. Her emotions ranged from complete shock to self-righteous indignation.

"You can't be serious," she finally muttered.

"I'm afraid this is the only way, Morgan, unless you want to see Sean in pain for days. He's certainly not about to let Skord do it. You're the only other vampire we've got right now. I can call in another from one of the other safe houses, but then a lot of explanation would be necessary. That might mean your secret and Pat's could be revealed…about not ever wanting to join the agency and become a vampire, that is."

Morgan took a deep breath, ran one hand over her face, and slowly shook her head. "He's going to owe me out his ass for this!"

Dani let out a relieved sigh. "Come on. Let's go to your bedroom…I'll help you get ready."

The entire time Morgan readied herself, she became

more and more anxious about what she was being asked to do. And how could Danielle or Skord expect that Sean would let her? Surely, he'd tell her to get her butt out of his room and leave him alone. And that'd come *after* using a few nasty nouns to describe her.

The anger he had concerning her refusal to follow orders wasn't going to end just because she was offering herself.

Worse…there was something about the way Dani kept smiling—a sort of sweetly wicked smile that made her want to pop somebody's lights out.

By now, the entire household had calmed down. No rogues had charged over the horizon, with eerie eyes gleaming, flesh rotting, or swords swinging. Morgan surmised this was why at least Dani's mood had changed for the better. *She,* however, groused on about this upcoming infliction on her personal space. "He's *so* gonna owe me…it won't even be funny," she repeated over and over. "I ought to charge his ass for the favor!"

As Dani ignored her tantrum and helped her get ready, the woman irritatingly hummed beneath her breath, as if nothing were wrong. Aggravated beyond measure, Morgan could do nothing to wipe the cream-guzzling grin from the older woman's face.

To be continued in the next book of the series and thank you for reading…

***

Continue this series with, **The Nightwatchers, "*Sean,*" Book 2**

by Candace Sams.

Get the link to the next book on Amazon

just type in the title and author name into Amazon's search engine as

(title, Candace Sams) or go to:

www.CandaceSams.com

About the Author

Candace Sams is a *USA Today Bestselling Author* who has published over a hundred novels. Some are now being vetted for movie options. She resides in a rural area of the USA, loves collecting Halloween paraphernalia, is a Master Gardener and adores all animals. She also loves to hear from readers. Find her social media contacts and newsletter link at:
www.CandaceSams.com

https://www.facebook.com/CandaceSamsAuthor/

https://twitter.com/CandaceSams

https://www.bookbub.com/authors/candace-sams

All books available through Amazon:
https://smile.amazon.com/Candace-Sams/e/B001USAELG?ref=sr_ntt_srch_lnk_1&qid=1559494414&sr=8-1

The Nightwatchers Series:

The Nightwatchers – Greenwood: Book 1
The Nightwatchers – Sean: Book 2
The Nightwatchers – Skord: Book 3
The Nightwatchers – Into the Night: Book 4
The Nightwatchers – Jamie: book 5

www.ingramcontent.com/pod-product-compliance
Lightning Source LLC
Chambersburg PA
CBHW061426150726
47987CB00001B/107
* 9 7 9 8 3 5 8 0 0 1 6 8 8 *